To Hanna

MANIC
ROOK + RONIN
BOOK TWO

To Sannon

MANIC
ROOK + RONIN
BOOK TWO

J. A. Huss

Copyright © 2014 by J. A. Huss

All rights reserved.
Second Edition

Edited by RJ Locksley
Cover design by J. A. Huss
Formatted by Tianne Samson with E.M. Tippetts Book Designs

E.M.
TIPPETTS
BOOK DESIGNS

ISBN-978-1-936413-74-4

This is a work of fiction. Names, characters, businesses, places, events and incidents are either the products of the author's imagination or used in a fictitious manner. Any resemblance to actual persons, living or dead, or actual events is purely coincidental.

BOOKS BY J.A. HUSS

Losing Francesca

Science Fiction Series

Clutch
Fledge
Flight
Range
The Magpie Bridge
Return

Rook and Ronin Books

TRAGIC
MANIC
PANIC

Rook and Ronin Spinoffs

SLACK: A Day in the Life of Ford Aston
TAUT: The Ford Book
FORD: Slack/Taut Bundle
BOMB: A Day in the Life of Spencer Shrike
GUNS The Spencer Book

Dirty, Dark, and Deadly

Come
Come Back
Coming for You (November 2014)
James and Harper: Come/Come Back Bundle

Social Media

Follow
Like
Block
Status
Profile
Home

TRAGIC is over and Rook is ready for the future—Spencer Shrike and the STURGIS contract!

It's three months of body art modeling! That means three months of Spencer Shrike's paintbrush all over her body, three months in front of Antoine's camera, and three months of twenty-four-hour filming for Spencer's Biker Channel reality show.

Wait a minute… what reality show? Maybe she should've read that STURGIS contract a little closer?

Sure, Rook's bank account is overflowing, but Ronin is angry, Clare is trying to escape rehab, Antoine is a worried mess, and Elise is just trying to hold everyone together. Rook's new family is about to fall apart before she even gets the chance to enjoy it.

ONE

ROOK

There's a cool breeze swimming up my bare legs and Ronin's feather-light touch just compounds the tickle. I try my best not to squirm, but I don't entirely succeed. I stuff my face into the pillow and stifle a giggle and I hear him sigh behind me.

"See?"

"See what?" I ask, half turning. "You're doing it that way on purpose. If that was Spencer, he wouldn't be *trying* to turn me on."

He squints down at me. I rest my gaze briefly on his eyes, those electric blue eyes. They are amazing. Actually, all of Ronin is amazing. His chest is… perfect. He's got very little hair on it and that's something I quite like. What I like even more is the little trail that trickles down the middle of his abdomen and disappears down his boxer shorts.

I realize my fingers just walked their way down to the waistband of his shorts right along with my eyes and when I look up at him he's grinning.

MANIC

"That's a naughty look on your face, Gidge."

I snicker and sit up. I'm wearing the blue nightie he gave me from the studio closet when I first came here. "You do that to me sometimes."

"Only sometimes?" He tackles me and rolls me over until I'm on top of him.

I know it's just your basic flirt, but actually, Ronin does it to me at all times. I have to take a deep breath to quiet my heart rate a little because everything about him sets me off. "Kiss me."

He does. He kisses me like he hasn't seen me in weeks. Months. Like he didn't just make love to me an hour ago. I embrace that kiss and drag my fingertips down his back. He takes the paintbrush in his hand and sweeps it slowly down my chest, making me buckle back.

He pulls me forward. "Oh, I like that," he moans in my ear. "But I don't like to think about Spencer having that effect on you at all."

"Ugh. You ruined it! I was just about ready to give in and you ruin it!"

He rolls us over again and places himself on top, in control. He holds me down by the wrists and then leans down and kisses my neck with little fluttery breaths that carry up into my ear and make me squirm. "I give! I give!"

He kisses my lips once, just a quick one, then rolls off me. "You're so ticklish, he's gonna be tickling you all up, Rook. I hate it."

I know he hates it and he's been so perfect pretending that he doesn't. He's been supportive and understanding about the whole mess. We finished the TRAGIC contract about a couple weeks ago, which was its own little nightmare with all the nude crack-whore pictures those people wanted, then went on a little mountain vacation up to Granby Lake for a week to try and forget the whole experience. I wonder if all contracts require a vacation to put it behind you?

I really hope not. Although I don't see myself taking another contract. I think I've had my fill.

I thought this whole body art stuff with Spence would be OK, but it is what it is. Sure, I'll look like I have clothes on when he's finished doing his thing, but the reality is—I won't have clothes on. I'll be completely, one hundred percent nude.

"Ticklish isn't the same thing as turned on, you know." I smile to try and make him feel better, but honestly, he has every right to be jealous and worried. Not because I'm going to do anything with Spencer. I'm not interested in Spencer at all. But the guy will have his paintbrush all over me.

Like *all* over me.

And if some girl was painting my boyfriend all up for the sake of making a walking billboard, yeah, I'd be pissed.

"Just because I wiggle a bit doesn't mean I want to have sex with him, Ronin." I say it gently because I'm so in the wrong in this one. I have nothing. I take my hands to his face and rub the stubble on his cheeks softly. "I know it bugs you, and I'm pretty sure I already regret signing this contract, but it's done. They've got it all set up, it's three months, then I'm out and we can make real plans. I'll go back to school and we'll make real plans." I kiss him and he responds with a half-hearted nibble on my lower lip.

Everything he said to me that day we finally opened up to each other is turning out to be true, and I figured he was right at the time anyway, I knew that. But I never expected to regret things so quickly. Right now I have more than fifty thousand dollars in my bank account. Accounts, actually, because Antoine took me to his accountant and they explained all sorts of money shit to me that made no sense, and then they told me to put my money here and there, and I signed the papers and then we went to a bank with some other money and I got a little plastic card with my name on it.

I've never had one before because Jon, my psycho ex, always kept the money in his name. So even though I have receipts in a folder that say I have accounts with many thousands of dollars in them, that card carries more meaning.

MANIC

Ronin was right. I don't need the money. But I had no idea that TRAGIC contract was paying so much. I really thought five grand was pushing it, but the total was actually fifty-seven thousand and it blew my fucking mind when I heard that number. Ronin got a bunch too, even Billy got some because he did that one shoot with me.

Maybe I'm not rich long-term, but I'm looking pretty good right now as far as money goes.

I laugh a little and Ronin makes a face. "What?"

"I have more money than I need, I think."

"Yeah," he sighs. "You just sock that shit away and don't touch it. Save it."

He's said this before and what he's really saying is that he's paying for everything and my money is no good here. Maybe that would've bugged me a few weeks ago, it might've felt like he was trying to control me, but Ronin's not like that. He's just trying to take care of me, and even though that was a huge red flag because of Jon's controlling ways, I think I'm coming around to it because he took care of everything during our lake trip, which was so much fun. We had this little cabin that we shared with Antoine and Elise in the forest and we rented a boat for a few days and went fishing. Which was really just everyone drinking beer and pretending we gave a shit about fishing.

Then we went to this little bar in the mountains that was famous for hosting big-name bands even though it was in the middle of nowhere. It overlooked the Poudre River though, and was a fantastic place. A local band played that night, but still, they were good and the shows were all ages, so it didn't matter that I wasn't twenty-one. There were two universities not very far away, so there were lots of college kids, and lots of underage kids like me. I watched them and wondered if I'd ever get my chance at school or if that would just remain a dream.

"For school," Ronin continues, like he's reading my mind. "UCLA is pretty expensive, but I think you'll have more than enough when this contract is up."

I'm not one hundred percent sure what this contract will pay, it depends on a few factors like total production costs. But if I got paid fifty grand for that stupid TRAGIC stuff which was less than two weeks' worth of work, then this should be a lot more. It's thirty painting outfits with thirty different bikes, plus the trip to Sturgis and the show up at some big campground venue.

"I don't have to go to UCLA, you know. It makes no difference to me where I go to film school. I mean, didn't those *South Park* guys go to Boulder? That's not far, right?"

"No, it's not too far to commute. I finished my degree up there after quitting DU to get away from Spencer. He transferred to Fort Collins to get away from me and I guess that's why he keeps his workshop up there. But you said UCLA, and if that's where you want to go, you should go. Don't let me stop you."

It hurts a little the way he says that. Like we're not quite in this together. Like it's just me going to LA. "Well, I have no chance of getting into any of those schools unless I put in at least two years of community college, so I guess that's a conversation for another day."

He pulls me close and kisses me on the cheek. "That's the best thing I've heard all morning. Two whole years of you in school, forced to stick around and fall in love with me."

I am so totally in love with Ronin Flynn right now, it's scary. He doesn't say the L word and neither do I, but I have never felt this way about a guy. Not even my first love, Wade.

I turn and rest my head on his chest. "This is a really good moment."

"Yeah," he breathes. "Let's go back to sleep and make it last a little longer."

My eyes close and we breathe in and out together like we're a team.

And the last thought I have as I drift off. I want us to be a team. We're not just a couple, we're a team.

TWO

ROOK

Pounding on the door wakes me just as Ronin slips out of bed and rushes down the hallway to take care of things. I ignore him and the pounding. Whatever's happening, it most likely doesn't involve me. I know we have a meeting with the STURGIS people today, but it's not until four and—I pause my internal monologue to look at the clock on Ronin's nightstand— it's only five-thirty.

I laugh.

Oh, well. So what? Don't stars get to be bitches and come in late and generally act like assholes towards all the little people who—

"Get your ass up, Rook! You're late!"

Guess not.

He rips the sheet off me and I shield my eyes from the blazing-ass sun that pours into the bedroom as he lifts the blinds. "Shit, Ronin. Give me a second."

He sighs. "The producer is pissed off and honestly, I'm not

MANIC

in the mood to fight your battles for tardiness. You signed, now you're in. So get up and get to work. They wanted permission to install the cameras in your apartment, they've been waiting down on the terrace for almost two hours, banging on the door. Finally Elise and Antoine got back from visiting Clare and came up here looking for us."

"Well, no one told them to show up early, and—hey, wait a minute. What cameras?"

He sneers down at me as he shakes his head. "How could you not know this?"

"What cameras?" I repeat slowly.

"The reality show, Rook, it was in the contract you signed. They get to follow you around for three months."

I sit up and shake my head. "No, Spencer said the show was about the STURGIS Rally, I'm sure of it. He said they were filming the rally for the kick-off, so why do they need cameras on me now?"

"Because, Gidge, it's a two-hour pilot that follows the whole process of Spencer painting the girl, that's *you*, and making the bike to match her."

"Oh."

"Get up and get dressed." He throws me some jeans and a t-shirt from his closet. "Hurry, this guy's a dick and he can dock your pay if you screw around."

"Well, fuck. The only reason I'm doing this is for the money."

"Right, so fall in line and do what you're told." And then he disappears in his closet and gets dressed.

"Fall in line," I mutter as I watch him. "I don't like that."

"No?" Ronin asks, coming out of the closet pulling on some boots. "Well, you're in the wrong business, Gidget. Because doing what you're told is pretty much the only way to succeed as a model." He pulls me up out of bed and smacks me on the ass. "Chop, chop, my little money-maker."

"You're funny today, Larue. I will definitely punish you for that crack later."

He leans in and kisses me on the neck as his hands cover my hips and sway me back and forth a little. "I can't wait. Now hurry, if we get this meeting over quick we can go grab dinner somewhere nice. I'll meet you down in Antoine's office."

And then he's gone in a rush. Say what you will about Ronin—I mean, he's a male model, he's somewhat bossy and controlling, and he's got some very Sixties opinions on what he's looking for in a wife—but he is not lazy. The man works his ass off around here. I guess I didn't notice it much during most of TRAGIC because I was too busy being confused and defiant, but he starts his day very early.

Ungodly early.

In fact, this whole studio is filled with those driven A-type workaholic personality people who live for their jobs. Granted, most of them go home, but Elise, Antoine, Ronin, and now me, we stay here twenty-four seven.

I'm not even remotely interested in investing so much of myself and my life in this stuff. Now, maybe if my job was film school or making movies, I might feel the same way.

That brings my attention back to the whole reality show thing. I did not read that contract, I skimmed it in a fit of rage after Ronin started a fight with Spencer and then I got knocked down to the ground by accident. I wonder if the cameras have to be in my bedroom?

That makes me want to throw up.

But I totally asked for this. This was my big declaration of independence. It was a temper tantrum of Rook pointing to herself and screaming, *Look at me, look at me! I'm in control now!*

What a dumbass I am. Seriously, what was I thinking? Taking all my clothes off for three months of nude body painting. I must've been on some serious instability emotions that night. I sigh as I pull on the clothes Ronin left. Everything is huge, but I've made a big deal about not moving my stuff up here to his apartment so I can retain my freedom. So it's either wear the dirty clothes from yesterday, or his stuff.

MANIC

I choose his stuff because it smells like him and his smell is delicious. I snicker at this as I brush my teeth and hair, then slip on my old Converse sneakers and head downstairs. The studio is empty today because they've scaled down the regular shoots for the summer. They still have a few jobs going, but no other contracts like STURGIS. They want me to have privacy so it's not weird, but that's pretty stupid since the cameras are gonna be there. My naked body will be on the Biker Channel next year.

I shudder at that.

Bikers staring. DVR-ing me.

Yuck.

I take the stairs down to Antoine's office slowly, listening to the conversation that leaks out. They're not saying anything important from what I can tell, but one guy who has a snooty clip to his speech sounds a little put out about me not being on time. I picture him in my head as my sneakers creep down the concrete steps. He sounds like he's wearing a suit.

When he comes into view as I turn the corner to head back to the office, I put the visual together with the voice.

Yup. He's a suit.

He watches me as I walk towards them, then Ronin, who has his back to me, turns and smiles. "There you are. See, told you, Ford, she's here, she's ready."

Ford—what a stupid name first of all—looks at me dubiously as I approach Ronin, who is now my manager. We decided this on vacation out at the lake. Elise said I had to have someone and I could either go get an agency to represent me, or hire my own manager. I hired Ronin. Of course, he's not taking money from me, but he's in charge of everything, which, yeah, sounds like I sorta just gave in and let him take control, but it's different. It's only for business.

Since Ronin feels the need to kiss ass with this Ford guy, I stretch out my hand and say, "Nice to meet you."

He glares at me from light brown eyes under his furrowed brows. He does eventually reach out and shake my hand, but it takes a few seconds for him to decide to do this. I look over at Ronin as we shake and he smiles. His smile says, *Be nice.*

"It's a pleasure to meet you, Rook," Ford says unconvincingly. "We were given permission to install the cameras in your apartment, so the crew is in the process of doing that now."

"Where's Spencer?" I ask after looking around. "And everyone else?" It's just me, Ronin, and this asshole named after a truck.

Ford checks his watch. "Well, Ms. Walsh, you're quite late, I made special reservations at an exclusive restaurant downtown to celebrate our partnership, so they all went ahead." Then he disdainfully looks down at my clothes and winces. "You'll need to dress."

My face heats up with embarrassment at how this man is treating me. "Who the hell—"

"She's got an outfit, don't worry," Ronin says, pulling me towards the dressing room. "We'll meet you there."

"What the hell was that?" I ask once we're safely on the other side of the dressing room doors.

"That was called a pissed-off client, Rook, and typically when people are paying you a lot of fucking money to do a job, you try to avoid the pissed-off client. He was never on board with you in the first place, said you were too young, but Spencer insisted and he had a clause in his contract that he was in charge of picking the canvas."

"The canvas." *Wow.*

"Come on, now, put on the game face. You're in the contract, but this guy is just looking for way to make you screw up and have to pay him a bunch of money, so if you want to keep the cash you just made for TRAGIC, you'll have to be on your best behavior. Got it?"

"Got it," I say as he hands me a pencil skirt, a crisp long-sleeved white shirt, and some low black heels. "This is what I'm wearing?" I'm a librarian. "Can I safely assume the accessories will include glasses on a chain and my hair in a bun? Should I shush people tonight?"

MANIC

These people have no middle. It's either sweet or trashy.

"Just put it on, OK? We don't have time. Just trust me for once, will ya? I've been dressing models for five years, I know what I'm doing."

I grumble, but after I put the outfit on and Ronin hands me a brush and a clip to keep my hair neat, I decide some librarians can be sexy and I'm definitely one of them. When I turn from the mirror he's exiting from the men's side of the closet buttoning up his shirt cuffs.

We smile at each other.

"I can't wait to get you in bed again," he growls.

"Why wait?"

He smacks my ass and pushes me out of the dressing room. "Be good tonight, it's important."

I smile at that as we hop down the four flights of stairs that lead to the parking garage and then get in his truck. I take a deep breath as we exit onto the busy street outside our building and say a little prayer that this contract was a good choice.

THREE

ROOK

The restaurant is at the top of a very tall building in downtown Denver. I have no idea what this building is called or anything else about it, but I don't dwell on it because as soon as we give the valet guy the truck, Ronin is practically dragging me to the elevator.

"Shit, Ronin. Calm down, will you? You're making me nervous."

"Sorry," he says, squeezing my hand. "Ford is pissed and that means Antoine is pissed, and not to sound like a jerk, but Antoine is pretty serious about the business side to the studio, it's got his name on it after all, so we try to keep clients happy and this is a huge contract, Rook. Huge. So play it cool, be nice, and smile sweetly. *Please*," he adds at the last second.

I've never seen Ronin so... *on*. I'm thinking about how I really don't know him that well when the elevator doors open and he places a calming hand against the small of my back and gently guides me forward. He talks to the maître d' in French and

MANIC

they laugh like they're old friends, and then we're led past all the other diners and into a private area. Spencer's boisterous laugh fills the room as we enter as all heads turn to us. Antoine stands and walks over and takes my arm to place me in a seat next to him. Ronin shakes hands with all the suits and Spencer as he walks around the table to find his chair across from me.

I look to my left and there's that Ford guy. I smile sweetly like I was told, then look past Antoine to Elise. She's prettied up in a dark red dress that looks like someone made it specifically for her tiny little frame. Her short blonde crop is gelled up to make little wisps of hair curve against her cheeks and forehead. She smiles at me and raises a glass, her champagne and dimples both sparkling at the same time.

She's adorable.

I pick up my champagne glass and raise it back, then take a sip and realize it's water.

Ford leans into me a little, making me pull back. "You're underage, right?"

I catch Ronin's glare across the table and put on the game face and talk in my sweetest voice. "So, tell me, Ford—is that a family name? Or did your parents just like trucks?"

Spencer spits out his beer all over another suit guy and barks out a laugh. "Oh, Rook, I think the next three months with you will be the best of my life."

I look over at Ronin and he's not happy. I look over at Elise and her dimples are gone. I try not to look at Antoine, and it's not that hard because he's directly to my right so all I have to do is look straight, but I don't need to see him because he leans down and whispers in my ear, "Behave, Rook."

I turn to Ford. "No, seriously, it has to be short for something, right?" I bat my eyelashes at him and the rest of the table settles down and starts talking again. "Tell me, I'm interested. I have an unusual name myself."

He smiles but it's so fake I want to tell him he needs to practice that shit in the mirror before he unleashes it on the world. "It's short for Rutherford. A family name, as you said."

"Nice," I say. "I'm named after a chess piece myself, the rook. You know what the rook does, Ford?"

He laughs a little. "Yes, Rook, I know. But Spencer told us you're named after a bird. Which was why he fell in love with you and insisted that you be the nude body he gets to paint up this summer."

He says the last bit as he looks at Ronin, and this makes my heart beat a little faster. What's going on here? "Well, that too," I say, watching Ronin stare at Ford. "Uh, do you guys know each other?"

"Oh, yeah," Spencer says from down the table. "Ford, Ronin, and I go way back. High school."

"Oh, Catholic high school, right?"

"That's right," Ronin says. "Ford was two years ahead of us."

"Uh-huh." I wait for Ronin to continue but he drops it and starts talking to the suit guy next to him.

I look up at Ford and he's smiling. But it's not a good smile and I feel a little protective of Ronin. It doesn't take a mind reader to get the fact that Ronin and Ford are not friendly.

There's like a team of waiters just for us and they appear and talk to each of us personally about what we want. They don't have hamburgers or grilled chicken salads here because this place has nothing but French food.

It's like my worst dining nightmare come true.

Ford gets something I can't even pronounce and Antoine chats in French with the staff and then chooses a whole bunch of shit I can't pronounce. Finally I look across the table at Ronin and he's smiling.

"Would you like me to order for you?"

"Please choose the hamburger," I say, grinning.

I'm pretty sure I'd understand hamburger in French, so I'm also pretty sure that's not what he gets me.

After the food is ordered Elise announces she needs to go to the restroom and then walks up next to my chair and waits. "Oh,

MANIC

you want me to go with? OK." I get up and know she's gonna chew my ass out in there. Ronin lifts up his glass and gives me a cheers as I look at him for help.

I suppose this is what I get for being mouthy.

She whooshes the ladies' room door open and right there in front of that towel person who stands around waiting for tips, she lays into me. "Do you have any idea what this contract is worth, Rook?"

I shake my head.

"Two point five million dollars."

I almost choke. "Elise, I'm sorry. But he's kind of a jerk. He's baiting me."

"He's baiting you," she says between clenched teeth, "because he wants you to screw up and forfeit the money. We got the contract, so as long as we fulfill it we get paid. But do you understand that he can dock us for things like being late?"

I shake my head.

"I'm only going to say this once. You work for us, you have a contract. You will be polite when you speak to him, he's your producer now. You will also be considerate of his time. Do you understand me?"

I nod like a kid and Elise hands the towel person a twenty-dollar bill and walks out.

I stare at the door as it whooshes closed and then look over to the attendant. She's a middle-aged woman in a tight uniform. "First time with the big shots?" she offers helpfully.

"Yeah."

"Yeah," she repeats as she pockets her tip in a crisp white apron. "Hope it's worth it."

I follow Elise out and find her taking deep breaths just outside the door. "OK, I get it. I'll shut up and do what I'm told."

She smiles. "Perfect. Now, please, use your talents for good, Rook. You're likable, he'll like you, just be nice. It's Ronin he hates, they've never been friendly, just tolerant." And before I can ask her about that she hooks her arm in mine and we walk back to the table like old friends.

Dinner is a boring nightmare from my perspective, but from Ronin, Antoine, and Elise's perspective, it goes swimmingly. Ronin gets me some kind of meat—duck, I think. He's too busy chatting with the suits to pay much attention to me. Duck is not really my thing, so I skip most of the main course and concentrate on being polite to Ford. Everyone leaves happy, my transgressions are forgiven, and it's not until Ronin gets into his side of the truck that I let out a deep breath. "That was no fun at all."

He gives me a long look, then puts the truck in gear and pulls out of the valet area. "I think you're going to be sorry for taking this contract, Rook, but there's nothing you can do right now. Even if you wanted out, they'd probably fine you."

"Fine me for what?"

"Breach, of course. You're stuck and just so you know, while we were all at dinner, those cameras went into your apartment. You're stuck for three months."

"Can't I just stay with you?"

"You don't get it, do you? You signed a contract, Rook. You agreed to be in the show and be the body painting model for Spencer. You also agreed to walk down the main drag at Sturgis with nothing on but a very small thong and what amounts to two band aids over your nipples. In addition, you will appear on stage naked in front of five thousand drunk bikers for the final show. So whether you like it or not, whether you want to do it or not—you're stuck. You signed up for this and they're gonna hold you to it."

I turn away and look out the window as we stop at the light in front of the baseball stadium. "I should've listened to you, right? That's what this is about. I should've taken your advice, let you make decisions for me."

MANIC

He drives forward at the green light and then eases us into the parking garage under the studio. He pulls into his spot and turns the truck off and we sit in silence. "Well, yeah. I would've told you to do something else. Less money, but less exposure, too. But," he says, taking my hand, "I have more bad news. I have to drive up to Steamboat tomorrow to see Clare. She's causing a whole bunch of trouble apparently and she needs some support. She's got a couple months left in treatment and if she leaves now, she'll just go back to it and we might never get another chance to save her again."

"How long will you be gone?" My heart suddenly feels heavy. "I don't want you to go."

He gets out of the truck and comes over to my side and opens the door. "You'll be OK, Antoine will take care of you. Elise is coming with me, but Antoine has to stay, of course."

We walk slowly to the elevator. "OK," I say. Because it's not like I have a choice in this. He's leaving to help Clare and I'm stuck here working on a job I probably never needed and very much do not want to do. "Can't I stay with you one more night?"

I expect him to agree. I mean, how could he deny me that?

"No, Rook. You have to stay in your apartment, babe. You have to or they'll fine you for that too. And look, I know it's hard, but it's temporary. Once this is over you won't take another contract without a lawyer, OK?"

"Yeah," I say as the elevator doors open and drop us off on the fourth floor. He walks me out on the terrace and over to my garden apartment door and we stop. "I'm done signing contracts."

"Good, Gidge. Because even though you hate it, I really do know what's best for you right now." He leans down and kisses me, his hands lingering for just a moment on my hips, then pulls back. "I have to go pack, but I'll come by in the morning and say goodbye before I leave, OK?"

"OK."

"The cameras are in every room except the bathroom, but

there's one outside the door—they wanted to be able to see you getting ready, I guess."

"Lovely."

"Just keep the door closed and you'll have privacy."

Great, so the only place in my tiny apartment where I can be alone is in my bathroom with that godawful claw-foot tub that I hate.

"You're gonna be OK?"

I sigh. "I'm sure I will, I mean, I'm not happy, but I'm gonna live, right?"

"No more contracts," he whispers as he kisses me again. "No more." I nod in agreement as he tears himself away and opens my door. "See ya in the morning, Gidge."

I give him a smile for being so helpful and concerned. "Later, Larue."

He laughs and walks back to the studio.

I go inside and find each and every camera. They are little mirrored dome things. I walk up to each one—three in the living room, one in the hallway outside the bathroom, and one just outside of the bedroom, pointing at my bed. I stick my tongue out at each one, then rearrange my bedroom furniture so that camera that thought it was gonna watch me sleep has a very limited view.

It might not give me total privacy, but at least that eyeball isn't beaming directly down on me anymore.

I change in the bathroom, then turn out the lights and lie in bed, totally creeped out.

FOUR

RONIN

Ford is waiting near the studio windows when I walk in, his back to me, his stick-up-his-ass posture as erect as ever. It's been years and still the sight of him makes me want to punch his face in.

"Where'd you find her?" he asks without turning around.

"She found me."

"What's wrong with her?"

"She's a nice girl, Ford. So stay back. She'll do her job, don't worry."

"I'm not worried. So, where are you off to?"

"Clare. She's in rehab up in Steamboat—"

"Again?"

"Shit, Ford. Way to be an asshole. Have a little sympathy."

"She's been broken for how long now, Ronin? Three years? More? Hell, maybe she was never right, did that ever occur to you?"

"This time's different. She just needs some support."

MANIC

"Like all the other times?"

"OK, I'm done here. You hate her, she hates you—shit, I hate you. I'll see you when I get back. And don't bother Rook, she's not handling things well right now." I don't wait for an answer, I just walk over to the stairs and head to my apartment.

"Feels like old times, don't you think?" Ford calls out after me.

"No, Ford. It doesn't." *Asshole.*

When I get to the top of the stairs I can hear Elise and Antoine arguing in French. I head over and punch the code on the door. They hear the beeping and immediately stop the argument. When I walk in Elise is so angry her face is bright red.

"God, what? Seriously, Elise? Stop it!"

"What's going on, Ronin? If this is part of one of your jobs, leave us out of it!"

"It's not! Antoine, tell her. This whole project is legit! I had nothing to do with it. Do you really think I want to work with Ford and Spencer? Shit, you guys are the ones who wanted the fucking contract! I'm the one who said no! Now my fucking girlfriend's stuck in the middle, she's got no idea what I used to do, and the whole fucking thing is about to blow up in my face! There's a lot of shit that really *is* happening, Elise, so I do not need you accusing me of shit that's not!"

She pours herself a shot from the bar and downs it, slamming the glass on the polished wood for emphasis. "If I find out the three of you are working again, I will turn you in. Do you understand? I will not risk everything we've built here for these stupid schemes you guys cook up!"

I take a deep breath because Elise is trippin' right now. She's got every right to be wary, pissed off, even. So I just try and remain calm so she'll get over it sooner. It's no use arguing with her, because she's right.

"And I'm not about to hang out here and watch," she says, looking at me. "I'm going up to Steamboat, so you assholes stay here and do your jobs." She looks over to Antoine. "I'll go save your niece."

She storms off and leaves us alone. Antoine wipes his face with his hands. "She's angry," he says in English. "She was not expecting Ford to be part of this deal."

"No, Antoine, she's pissed. I had no idea Ford was in on this shit either, Spencer never told me dick and he told Rook even less. And look, I love Clare just as much as you guys do, but I'm obligated to help Rook for this contract. I have to be here for her."

"Ronin, please. You're the only one Clare listens to. Give it a few days, that's all. Just a few days of your time to see that she's getting the care she needs and she's on her way back to us."

I sigh. How the hell can I say no to that? I mean, this guy—he picked Elise and me up after our lives fell apart. He's been there for me since I was ten years old. And even though I've never thought of him as a father, or even a brother for that matter, he's the closest thing I have to family aside from Elise.

"And keep an eye on Ellie for me. She's got her opinion on this job and she's not letting it go."

"Why, though? I mean, where'd she even get the idea?"

He sneers at me. "Please, Ronin. The last time the three of you were together I bailed you out of jail."

"Hey." I throw up my hands in an innocent gesture. "Those charges never stuck." And before I can stop it, before I can hold it together to prove that I'm not that guy anymore and Elise has nothing to worry about, I grin.

No.

I chuckle.

Antoine sneers again. "You better stop that right now, Ronin."

I grin wider. "You have to admit, it was perfect, wasn't it?"

And even though Elise would verbally castrate him if she was here and saw it, Antoine grins widely as well.

Because Spencer, Ford, and I got away with a whole load of shit back in college.

And if we wanted to, we could do it again.

FIVE

ROOK

I wake up to Ronin's kiss.

"You came," I croak out in a sleepy voice.

"You doubted me? Rook, please. You should know me better by now. I'm reliable."

I open one eye and snort. "Maybe with most things, but not when it comes to Clare. Every time you ditch me it's for her."

"Not true. I never ditched you, I just have to take care of things. Antoine's been good to me, Clare is his niece, and all that aside, I like her. When she's not high and freaking out like a psycho, I like her. She's nice and she's funny. You'll like her too, Rook. Once she gets well again, I mean."

"Maybe," I say, but that declaration doesn't make me feel any better. In fact it makes me feel worse.

"Love what you've done with the place, by the way."

I open my eyes and remember the cameras. "Yeah, well, I'm good at getting by, right? I'm sure they can still see me over here in the corner, but at least it's not in full-on spy mode anymore."

MANIC

He kisses me again and then gets up. "You're leaving already?"

"Gotta go, sorry. Elise is already down in the garage waiting for me. I'll call you when we get there. Keep your phone on you, OK?"

I nod and then he's gone.

And I'm pretty sad about that. Even though I've been telling myself for months now that I'm number one, I don't need anyone, and settling back down is the worst possible option for me, I'm starting to have doubts.

Ronin is nice. He's more than nice, he's good. Not everyone is good, but these people are. I can feel it. Sure, Antoine is a jerk sometimes, and it pisses me off that he mostly speaks French and makes Ronin translate, but he's still been pretty cool. I should probably make an effort to learn some French, that way he could talk to me like he does Billy in a mixture of both languages, because it's obvious he only speaks English when he has to.

And even though Elise is a real hardass, she's nice too. She's firm when she has to be and gentle when she thinks I need it. I could do a lot worse in the world than these people, even if they make their money off erotic modeling. I'm one of them now anyway, right? I'm an erotic model. I haven't looked online, but Ronin did and he said those TRAGIC photos hit Japan a few days ago. That's where those TRAGIC people were from. The photos were for serial book covers and the first one with the cherry tree shoot is already for sale. There's ten in all and they are releasing the story in parts. Each week a few chapters go out with a picture of me on the cover. From Sweet to Tragic, that's the theme.

Hopefully the books flop and no one reads them and sees me on the covers, but with my luck I'm sure this author is the Japanese version of EL James. At least they are confined to Asia right now. Ronin said they have no immediate plans to distribute the books in the US, so, phew. Dodged a bullet there.

I laugh at this because it's ridiculous to be worried about my body on the cover of erotic romances in Asia making their way over here when I'm about to be photographed naked with thirty bikes. This will probably turn into full-page ads in major motorcycle magazines, maybe billboards around freaking Denver for Spencer's shop, not to mention the nude walk of shame down the Sturgis strip and the private performance to end the rally in August. And then I get the pleasure of reliving every moment in hi-def on the Biker Channel next spring.

I decide to let all this shit go. What can I do? The contract is signed, the painting starts tomorrow, this is my last day off for three months. I should go back to sleep and enjoy it.

I take my own advice and pull the covers back over my head.

No one pounds on my door today. No one calls on my new iPhone I bought with all my new money either. But it's only four PM, maybe Steamboat is a long drive? I grab my phone and bring up the Internet, then type in 'drive time from Denver to Steamboat'.

It says about four hours. He should've been there by lunch.

I drag myself up, then barely catch myself before undressing in front of the camera. I sneer up at my spies and grab some clothes and go in the bathroom to clean up and dress.

The studio is busy but not bustling too bad for a Monday. Usually it's crazy busy, but this STURGIS contract is taking up the whole summer, so I guess Antoine had to cut back on other stuff. I do catch a glimpse of Billy and he waves from across the room. I wave back. He's not as bad as I thought. Ronin and I went out with him and his on-again off-again girlfriend a few times. If you picture what kind of life a male model lives, Billy fits that stereotype perfectly.

Ronin is the complete opposite. He's not a big drinker, he

MANIC

doesn't do any drugs at all, but he does gamble a little at a place in the mountains called Black Hawk. That place is not far—I know because I've gone with him once. I'm not twenty-one, so pretty much all the fun stuff up there is off limits to me.

It sucks being underage when all your friends aren't.

Antoine and Spencer are chatting next to a bike on the far side of the studio and when Antoine sees me, he waves a hand, gesturing me to come over.

"Hey, Rook," Spencer says as I approach.

"Hey, what's up with you guys today?"

"This is our first bike, Rook," Antoine says. He points to the Shrike bike. It's not anything extraordinary, so I'm not sure what I'm supposed to do with that information.

"Cool," is about all I can manage.

"We'll photograph this bike tomorrow, just the one," Spencer says. "So you and I can get used to each other. It'll probably take me most of the day to get the artwork right, then Antoine will want to fuck with the photo gear, so just one bike tomorrow. But we're hoping we can do more than one for each session after that."

"Oh? Sounds like a lot of hours."

"It will be," Antoine says. "Long days, but Spencer's decided he can be more efficient with his projects, use the base paint and only change the colors on some, to get the catalog shots over with quickly."

"Yeah," Spence chimes in, "I need to get the fuck back to Fort Collins and work on the Raven on the weekends, so the sooner we can get these catalog shots done, the better it'll be. I have a lot of work to do still. Plus, I need to spend some time on the final design for your body. After painting you up for the catalog shots I'll be pretty familiar with it, so I can plan better."

"Uh-huh, sure. Sounds like a plan to me."

"So what we were thinking, Rook"—Antoine picks it up again—"is that we'll shoot for a week getting as many bikes down as we can, then take the weekends off while Spencer works up at his shop."

I shrug. "OK." I mean, really, like I have a choice? I'm the hired help. I'm a walking billboard sign.

I leave them there talking about bikes and stuff and hop down the stairs to get some food from Cookie's. I don't know why I continue to go over there, I have a ton of money and I could eat anywhere I want, but I like that place. And it reminds me of Ronin. I miss him already. I sigh as I press the button at the crosswalk that leads to the diner, then wait for the light to change before making my way across the street.

I enter the diner and the hostess is Cindy. She recognizes me and nods, so I take that as I'm a regular now and I can seat myself at the back booth that is reserved for Ronin's girls. God, how that bugged me when I first met him. Having to come in here and declare that I belonged to Ronin was humiliating, especially since all that stuff with Jon was so fresh.

I feel better about it now, plus I don't say that anymore. I don't have to. They know I belong to Ronin.

I grin at that as I take my seat, then grab a menu and start looking it over for something different. A shadow appears at my booth and I'm just about to tell the waitress I'd like the turkey club on a Kaiser roll when I realize it's Ford.

"Can I help you?" I ask rudely, then check myself and smile.

He smirks back and takes a seat across from me. "Rook, I had no idea you enjoyed diner food."

He's dressed in a suit, just like he was last night, and his day wear looks just as expensive as his evening shit. "Ditto, Ford. You look like a French restaurant kinda guy to me."

Cindy does appear then and I order the club while Ford asks for a coffee.

"What do you want?" I ask.

He tsks his tongue. "Why are you so combative with me?"

If this asshole thinks he's gonna win this little game of wits with me, he's mistaken. I might not be college-educated and produce reality shows—*yet*, I secretly say in my head—but I'm not a fool either. "Look, Ford, I already know you never wanted

MANIC

me on the show, so save it. I know you don't like me."

I pretend to people-watch and ignore him as Cindy brings him a coffee.

"Well, that's not what's going on here, Rook," Ford says after Cindy leaves. "I do like you. You're pretty to look at, that's for sure. And I know that Ronin and Spencer both like you, so why would I not like you?"

"Then why are you being a jerk to me?"

"When was I a jerk?"

"*Oh, Rook,*" I say in a fake voice, "*You're underage, right? So sad, you have to drink water at dinner.* Save it, OK," I say, returning to my normal voice. "Because I already know you don't want me on the project. You think I'm too young."

He smiles and it disarms me for a second. He's got nice teeth. *Teeth, Rook?* I shake my head a little as he starts talking again. "You *are* too young. If I were Ronin I'd forbid you from doing this contract."

"Forbid me? Pfft. Ronin is not in any position to forbid me from doing anything."

"No? I thought the two of you were together."

"If you mean are we dating, then yes. But he's not my keeper, Ford. I make my own decisions, thank you."

We sit in silence for a while. He looks around, interested in anyone but me, so I take out my phone and check for missed texts and voicemail. It's pointless, I have the ringer on and it never went off, but I check anyway to pretend like I have something else to do besides talk to Ford. I'm the modern-day version of the girl sitting by the phone. I snort a little at that, because pining women have come a long way if you think about it. We can go out and have fun and impatiently wait for our boyfriends to call all at the same time.

Cindy appears again and slides my plate over to me. Ford is still nursing his coffee and covers the top of it with his hand to keep her from filling it back up. I thank Cindy and then start eating. I feel like a starving lumberjack. I barely ate any of that

French shit last night at dinner and then I forgot to eat when I got home. Add in my missed breakfast and I have to stop and thank my lucky stars Ronin didn't want to weigh me this morning. I probably lost a few pounds. He's a total freak about the models losing weight and if it's me losing I can only imagine the freakout would triple.

"So let me get this straight." Ford continues the conversation from ten minutes ago, like he's been pondering my answer the whole time. "Ronin is your boyfriend but he's not allowed to tell you not to do harmful things?"

I shrug. "Yeah, I guess. We're dating but he's not my father, Ford. I think I can identify harmful things just as well as he can." This is a total lie. I was stuck in an abusive relationship for three years and the guy almost killed me before I finally figured out I needed to leave. But I don't want Ford to know any of that, so I play it cool and just take a bite of my sandwich.

"Hmmm…"

"Hmmm, what?" I say with my mouth full. Maybe I can gross him out and make him leave me alone.

"You're close to his type, but not quite."

What's this guy's deal? "OK," I say, still chewing. "I'll play. What's his type, Ford? If I'm not it, then what's he usually go for?"

"Clare. She's his type, Rook."

"Oh, well"—I swallow—"something tells me the whole junkie thing's not working for him these days."

"No doubt. But she wasn't always a junkie. She went to school with us for a while my senior year. Her mom died and her father wanted her to go to school in the US, so Antoine let her come for a summer and then decided to keep her here. She and Ronin have been tight for a long time now. He crushed on her hard for a while back in school. Then Mardee came along. He wanted her more, I suppose, so Clare was forgotten. But they're all forgotten eventually, so Mardee became just another junkie. He likes the lost ones, Rook. He likes to swoop in and save them. Or think he's saving them, because let's face it, his track record is

MANIC

pretty bleak. But you have a little more sense to you, and I always thought Ronin liked the dumb ones, you know? The ones who don't know any better. Or the young ones."

I just stare at him with my mouth open.

"You come off as pretty smart, plus you don't seem to have any life issues that he can fix, so I just can't picture the two of you together. The only thing that interests him is your age from what I can see. Unless you have some secret fucked-up life I don't know about."

"Wow, Ford, you're a total asshole, aren't you?"

"If you say so," he says, continuing on like my opinion of him hardly matters. "I guess it shouldn't surprise me that he's allowing you to do these nude modeling contracts because that makes you need him. He's your manager, right?"

"You know he is," I sneer.

"Well, if you were dating me," he says standing up and reaching for his wallet. "I'd forbid it. It wouldn't even be up for discussion. And if you did go and sign a contract without counsel, one that required you to pose nude several dozen times, I'd have ripped Spencer a new asshole if he didn't talk you out of it." He throws a twenty down on the table as he waits for my reaction.

"Food's free here," is all I have to say.

"Nothing's free, Rook."

And then he walks out.

SIX

ROOK

Ford's words sting. Like bad.

Because not only am I young, too young to do anything fun with everyone else Ronin hangs out with, I'm also pretty fucked up in the life department. I mean, that was my whole deal, right? I was tragic. So tragic they had a campaign with my name on it. So fucking tragic I was living in a homeless shelter when I turned up here.

My appetite is gone after four bites of my sandwich and my stomach roils with the thought of eating anything else right now. I grab my phone off the table and leave the diner, walking slowly back to the studio. The doors are locked since it's after hours so I key in my code and then start to walk up the stairs, but change my mind and take a seat on the bottom step. I can hear a whole bunch of shit going on up there—lots of people here still. But I feel pretty alone.

I basically have no friends.

I have Ronin, but he's a boyfriend, so I'm not sure if that

MANIC

counts. Plus he's far away.

I have Elise, but she's more like a boss than anything else. Plus she's far away too.

I have Antoine, but he's… I don't even have another relationship to compare Antoine to. I can't even imagine in my wildest dreams of approaching Antoine and asking him if he wants to catch a movie or something.

None of the other models talk to me. Val, that tiny blonde girl who walks around naked every chance she gets, is sorta nice. But she's never asked me if I wanted to do anything after work. Plus, she's on vacation with almost everyone else while we do this STURGIS contract.

Billy is OK, but I'm too young to participate in his brand of fun.

Spencer is really cool actually, but he's running like four companies. He's got a bar, the Shrike Bikes, the TV show, and the painting. He's got no time to be my friend.

And that's pretty much it as far as my social circle goes. It's pathetic. And even though Chicago holds the worst memories of my entire life, I suddenly wish I was there so I could at least attempt to look up an old friend. Maybe Stacy Juniper who was my foster sister for almost a year at one house. Or even some of my old foster parents. They didn't all hate me, some of them just had bad luck, not enough time or money to keep other people's kids. Stuff like that.

It's dangerous to have only one friend, who in this case for me is Ronin. Dangerous because you start to depend on them too much.

"Rook! There you are," Antoine calls from above. "Come up to the third floor, we have to go over the show details."

"Yeah, OK." I drag my ass upstairs and when I get to the third floor it's just Ford, Spencer, Antoine, and me.

"Are we ready, then?" Ford asks me.

"Sure," I reply, even though I have no idea what we should be ready for.

"OK, command central for the show is down here." He waves his hand and we all walk forward, then Antoine opens the door and waits until we all enter before pulling it closed behind him.

It's a huge room, not as big as the studio upstairs, and the ceilings are only ten feet tall instead of two stories, but it's still pretty big. There's nice light coming through the windows even though it's starting to get dark outside, and there's a table and a shit-load of art supplies packed onto of one of those red tool boxes professional mechanics have.

"This is where I'll do all the painting, Rook," Spencer says. "So you can have some privacy, then when I'm happy with the art, we'll go upstairs to shoot."

I nod out an OK.

"Over here, Rook"—Ford takes over—"is the production center for the show. All painting sessions will be recorded."

For the first time I notice there's a whole team of people over on the other side of the room. There's also a massive bank of monitors, wires going everywhere, camera equipment, and microphones. I look back to the guys and Ford continues.

"Each of you will have a team assigned. Antoine gets team one, Spencer gets team two, and Rook gets team three. I won't even tell you their names, they don't exist. If you need anything, you ask me. That guy over there sitting at the console"—I look and a big guy wearing a black Metallica T-shirt waves to us—"is our director, Larry. Larry runs pretty much everything but you three. You shouldn't ever need to talk to him, but he'll be talking to me to make sure we're making something people will want to watch when we're done."

I stop listening after that. I just smile and nod. *Uh, huh*, I tell them. *Sure, yes, I totally have it. No problemo. I'm in. Yes, sounds about right.* I give Ford every meaningless affirmation I can think of because I do not give one stupid shit about this show.

Basically what he said was, I have three dumbasses who get to follow me everywhere. Two cameramen and a sound guy. Plus Ford, because what kind of fun would this be if Ford

MANIC

wasn't tagging around all day long? Of course, Ford assures me he won't be around all the time—sometimes Antoine will need him or Spencer might have a question, but I'm probably the one who will need his guidance the most, you know, because of how young I am.

He is such a dick.

The only bright spot of this whole meeting is the revelation that my crew is not allowed in my apartment, but that's only because they have it all wired up anyway, so there's no point in cramming us all in that small space.

When I'm all out of nods and Ford is finally tired of hearing himself talk, I am excused.

By this time it's nine o'clock and Ronin never called me. And since Ford was so thoughtful this afternoon when he informed me I'm not Ronin's type, Clare is, I think the worst. I end the day sitting all by myself on my bed, literally huddled in the corner as I try to stay out of the camera. *Tomorrow,* I tell myself, *tomorrow will be so much better than today.*

Today is just a day that had a lot of new stuff in it, a day filled with confusing things, so it felt weird and scary.

But tomorrow those things will be less new, so I'll be less confused and it will be so much better than today.

At least I tell myself that.

But it's a lie and even my damaged psyche understands this, because tomorrow I will be naked in front of all of them and I'm sure, even compared to the whole groping experience I had with Billy that first time I did anything here at Antoine Chaput's erotic art photography studio, this will be scary as hell.

Because this time I know exactly what's happening.

And I signed on for every single second of it.

SEVEN

RONIN

"She didn't respond to the buprenorphine treatment."

That's it. That's all this asshole doctor says. Like I know what the fuck this drug is and what it means that Clare's not responding to it. I want to punch his fucking face in.

I take a deep breath instead. "Can you explain that to me? I'm not quite sure what it means."

"Oh," he says with a smile. "Sorry, I just figured you'd be familiar with treatment. Sorry."

I stop listening for a second because I'm pretty sure this fuckwad just insulted me. Just assumed because of who I am, I'd be a drug addict, too. Elise grabs my arm and shakes me.

"… but she's a heavy user, so we think a long-term methadone taper would work better."

"Right. So what's the problem? Put her on it."

"She's refusing. She might need to leave. She's playing with us, Mr. Flynn. She thinks she can force us to give her euphoric levels of opiates to relieve her withdrawal symptoms, so she's

MANIC

refusing everything. She's thrown herself into rapid detox four times in the last two weeks, then accepts the methadone to come out of it, and it starts all over again. This is not what we do here. In fact, her manipulation is unacceptable."

I rub my face with my hands. Now I just want to strangle Clare. "Where is she?"

He points down the hallway. "Room 23."

"Wait here, Elise." I disentangle Elise's clutching hand from my arm and head down the hallway. I knock once, then walk in.

The TV is blaring People's Court and Clare is slumped over in bed, obviously high off her ass from a large dose of opiates. "Well," I say in a soft whisper. "It's gonna pretty hard to have a conversation with you if you're constantly fucked up."

Her head slowly tilts in my direction. "Help me, Ronin."

I sit down on the bed and push her hair away from her hollowed and black-ringed eyes and my heart hurts for her. This is so difficult, I hate seeing her this way. She looks nothing like the girl who came to live with us in tenth grade. All I see is Mardee, the day before she overdosed. Clare tugs on my heart in so many ways. It kills me to see her like this, but it's a pain that I'm ready to let go. I can't take it anymore. "I'm trying, sweetie. I'm trying. But you're being bad. They might kick you out and seriously, Clare. You can't come home if they kick you out."

Her head rolls to the side and the tears spill out. "It hurts."

I've never taken drugs. Like ever. I'm probably the only fucking person alive who's never smoked a joint. Hell, even Antoine and Elise toke up every now and then. But I've never had the desire. I don't understand this not wanting to get better. I'm clueless. I've read the pamphlets that tell me this is out of her control. Her body chemistry has been changed by the drug and she can't fight it. It's too powerful.

But I still don't get it.

"Clare, they're gonna put you on a new treatment and you will agree to it, do you understand me? I can't fucking take this anymore. Why do you *want* to be sick?"

"It hurts!"

"Yeah, that fucking sucks. But you know what? Who gives a shit? It's either take the hurt or die. Do you understand that? You either take it or *die*."

"I'd rather die." And then she turns away and mumbles it again. "I'd rather die."

She calls my bluff. Because I can't let her end this way. I can't. I get up and walk out, heading back towards Elise and Dr. Assface, and come in at the middle of a conversation about getting Clare to sign new consent forms. "Mr. Flynn, I was just explaining to your sister that if she had family members here to make sure she signed all the consent forms and followed the program, we'd consider letting her stay."

Elise looks at me, her eyes pleading. "Please, Ronin. I've had enough. I can't watch another girl die from this shit. I can't do it." Assface walks off mumbling something about privacy and I run my hands through my hair as Elise continues. "I've seen too many girls go down this path, I've had it, Ronin. We need to *make* her get help. If we stay, she'll listen. We can drag her though this program, she'll get better."

"And then what, Elise? When she gets back to Denver and she's got all her fucking friends taunting her with drugs? It'll start all over again."

"Just let Antoine and me handle that part, OK? But I need you to stay here, Ronin. She's always listened to you."

"Rook is just starting her contract, Elise. I can't stay up here in the Buttfuck Mountains. I need to get back, she's got a shoot tomorrow and I'm her manager."

"Rook is not dying, Ronin. Rook is getting her picture taken. She signed that contract, you told her not to. So if she's big enough to make that decision, she's big enough to deal with the repercussions. Teach her a lesson about signing shit just to spite you."

And Elise is right, of course. Rook asked for this, she wanted to do it. She made a big deal about it. It was her decision. "But she

MANIC

never really understood the deal, Elise."

"Yeah, like I said. Repercussions for being stupid. Clare made stupid decisions too, and if Rook was in dire need, I'd say fine. Put her first. But Clare is family and she is *dying*, Ronin. If you walk away from her I'll never forgive you."

And there it is. The ultimatum. Rook or Elise.

And as much as I hate to do it, I choose Elise. Because what choice do I have? What choice do I have? This tiny woman is my only true blood family left.

EIGHT

ROOK

Even though I woke up several times during the night remembering to squish myself up against the wall to avoid the camera in my bedroom, I'm ultimately sprawled out, ass cheek fully exposed from my crooked shorts in the morning.

Note to self: Wear pants to bed from now on.

I'm annoyed, tired, and in no mood to fight the pathetic excuse for a shower that is my claw-foot tub sprayer system, so I grab some clothes and head over to Ronin's apartment to take a shower in the Beast. It's early, barely five AM, but Chaput Studios will wake soon because these people are morning freaks. How in the world can Spencer be a morning person? I mean, I can see Ford getting up at the butt-crack of dawn, he's got one of those sketchy A-type personalities, I bet. But Spencer?

Nonetheless, there are a bunch of people already in the studio when I enter and make a mad dash for the stairs that lead up to the apartments. I spy the camera crews and several of the guys—Team Rook, from the panicked look on their faces—scramble together their equipment.

I run down the hall, press in Ronin's door code, and rush inside before they can catch me. It's stupid, I know, they'll get enough footage of me this summer to embarrass my non-living relatives from the grave, but I can at the very least have an hour of personal time with Ronin's better-than-sex shower.

The control panel running the multitude of shower heads might as well be in French, that's how much sense it makes to me, but I push several buttons and enough jets come to life to manage a few minutes of relaxing hot water.

I'm showered and dressed far too quickly, but the clock says it's been almost forty-five minutes, so I make my way down to the studio where everyone is standing around looking at me when I appear. They have a buffet table with food on it and just about everyone has a plate filled with fruit and pastries.

Spence walks up to me and I try out a forced smile, so, so nervous about what's about to happen. "Hungry, Rook? Grab some chow and we'll get started in about twenty minutes. I've already eaten, so I'll meet you down in the art room, OK?"

And then the only friendly face leaves me there, his camera team scurrying to keep up with him. Now I'm alone with Ford and my "crew."

Ford smiles.

I go grab a plate and pile on some grapes, because the pastries are apple and I hate apple pastries. I think they expect me to go chat with them, but I take my stuff outside instead. The air is still very cool and that is definitely something I enjoy about Colorado. The summer nights are almost never hot. I cop a seat at one of the picnic tables and don't look over my shoulder when the doors open and my team appears. They stand around me, one guy holding a long stick with a microphone on it, the other two filming.

They don't say hi, and I guess that's normal, we're not supposed to interact with the crews. So I just ignore them and try to eat my grapes. The door opens again and I look back, hoping it's Antoine, but it's not. It's Ford.

He bellows out, "Good morning, Rook! Ready for today? I can't wait to get started!"

I bet he can't. I mean, he gets to gawk at my naked body all day, what's not to like?

"Oh, and by the way, no sneaking off to Ronin's apartment. That's a breach of contract. If we had cameras in there, then you could go about your business, but Ronin refused." He gives me a shrug that says, sorry, out of my control.

I ignore him.

"Oh, come on. You have to talk, that's in the contract too. You agreed to interact."

I get up, dump my plate into the trashcan near the door, then go back inside and make my way downstairs. The crew scurries along after me, but when I look back as I make the third floor, Ford is gone. I smile a real smile for the first time since Ronin left.

Spencer is whistling as he sets out all his art supplies and he's got his own camera crew, so now we're eight people in this place. Spence catches me sighing and squeezes my shoulder. "Want some tunes, Rook? I like to listen to music when I paint."

"Sure, put on whatever you normally listen to."

"Comin' up." He plugs his iPod into a speaker tower and messes with it for a few seconds. "This is what I call my *Gettin' Ready for Sturgis* playlist."

"Yeah? Who's on it?"

"Oh, everyone good, man. Deep Purple, some Zeppelin, some Priest, Sabbath, Seger, Skynyrd... you name it, I've got it."

I laugh. "I'm not really up on all the cool kids' music these days, but I know an old fart playlist when I hear it." His jubilant mood degrades into something somber, maybe even hurt—so I

MANIC

backpedal. "Uh, well, I like Freebird."

He shoots me with his finger. "There you go, Blackbird. Freebird suits you. I'll put the whole *Pronounced...* album on."

"Well, shit, that's like a whole day's worth of music right there."

He laughs. "You're a lot smarter than you let on, Rook. Ford over there better be careful with his baiting."

It takes all my self-control to ignore that creeper Ford. He deserves my undying indifference. "So Spence, how is it you're twenty-two and you still call it an album?"

Lynyrd Skynyrd blares through the tower and Spence turns it down to a conversational level. "Twenty-three, but I got a vinyl collection that would make your grandfather cry, Rook."

I sigh again. Thank God for Spencer. He's a good guy, he's easy-going, and he's happy. All three very good qualities when he's gonna have his paintbrush all over my body in like twenty minutes.

"OK, you ready then?"

I'm not really, but that's not the answer they're looking for. I try for words, I really do, but all I can manage is a gulp and a nod.

"Here," Spencer says, holding out a short white robe for me. "Just go get undressed and put this on, and twist your hair up or something, keep it out of the way."

I grab the robe and follow his pointing finger to a partition that has concept drawings tacked to it and is doing double duty as a makeshift dressing room for me. When I go behind it, I can still see everyone, and they can still see me, because this thing only goes up to my neck.

"Well, that's not quite privacy, is it?" I say to no one in particular. Which is good, but no one in particular is paying any attention to me, except for my camera crew who seem to think they get to follow me in here. I smack the microphone away. "Get the hell out. You'll see my goods soon enough, you assholes."

They back off, still filming, microphone hovering above.

"Rook," Ford starts in, "I won't tolerate things like that. So please, just be amicable."

Amicable, my ass. But he's right, it's not their fault I made a bad decision. "Sorry," I say as I strip out of my shorts and tank, tie the robe around me, then twist up my hair in a makeshift bun. I have sixteen eyeballs waiting anxiously for me, so I put on a brave face and step out from behind my partition.

Spencer comes over and takes my hand. "OK, it's gonna be weird, I get it. But Rook, I swear, this is just a job for me. OK?"

I nod.

"Besides, today is the catsuit, so what I'm gonna do is spray you up in black, so even though you'll be naked, you won't *feel* naked. Once the paint goes on, Rook, it feels different. Trust me, OK?"

"I do, Spencer. I trust you."

He smiles. "Good." And then he turns and walks over to Ford and they whisper to each other for a few seconds. Ford looks past Spencer's head and eyes me suspiciously, then nods an agreement.

"OK, both crews, let's take five. Rook," Ford says as he eyeballs me, "this is the only time we'll do this. Understand? The whole point of the show is to watch the girl get painted up naked."

I say nothing because I'm not sure what he agreed to, and even if it's what I think it is, I don't want to let him know I appreciate that, because he's a jerk.

When the room is cleared, Spencer motions me over to stand on top of a white canvas drop cloth and then turns to grab his airbrush. "OK, disrobe, girl. I'm ready. He's not gonna ask to come back in, right? He's just gonna have them sneak in. So how about you face the back of the room and I'll keep an eye on the door? That way, if they do their job right, you won't even notice when they come back in. Deal?"

"Deal." I let the robe drop. I'm not as scared as I was a few weeks ago of getting naked—those last few TRAGIC shoots cured me of that—it's just I hate the thought of men leering at me in person. And I don't even have Elise here today to keep an

MANIC

eye on me. She was a big comfort through all the other shoots. And when she wasn't there, Ronin was. Now they're both gone.

Spencer doesn't do anything stupid like whistle or even stare, he just primes his airbrush on a piece of cardboard, then begins spraying my body. I watch, fascinated at how my skin soaks up the paint. The mixture of color and air makes a cool breeze across my skin and I shiver, which is sorta unfortunate since I'm naked, but what can you do.

I catch Spencer smiling as he takes note of my new perkiness.

"So you *are* a man," I say with a grin.

He looks up at me with a wink, but true to his declaration of professionalism, keeps his mind on his work. He asks me to lift my arms, and I do, but besides that he is silent. I stay still and he makes his way around me. Spraying up and down my legs, a few long swipes of air across my nether regions, which are smooth because Elise made me get a thorough waxing a few days ago. She even waxed up my arms. I'm hairless everywhere except my head.

And then Spencer starts on my backside.

It's not that hard really, and Spence was totally right. Now that my body is covered in black paint I don't feel so exposed. He kneels down and asks me to spread my legs a little, then his paint goes up and down my inner thighs.

It's sorta erotic.

In fact I have to bite my lip at this one and I am so glad I'm facing the wall, because Ford and the crews came back in a while ago. That's all I need—Ronin watching TV next spring and figuring out this was almost a turn-on. It's not really my fault, having my body all squirted up with paint is a new sensation, and it's getting done in front of a whole crowd of people to boot. Not that I'm an exhibitionist or anything, but let's be real.

"OK, daydreamer. You can put your arms down and relax for a few minutes. I gotta mix up some colors and then we'll get started on the zippers and make the whole thing slutty as hell."

I surprise him with a laugh. "Gee, Spence, I can't wait." When

I turn around the first thing I see is Ford. He's sitting in a chair not five feet from me. It's a bit of a shock, but the nosy camera guys take my mind off Ford. They are zooming in on my tits. I roll my eyes. "You boys are so predictable." The camera pans up to my face and I decide to tell the audience a thing or two. "I mean, am I right, girls? All these assholes think about are tits."

I chance a glance at Ford and he shoots me a thumbs-up. I get a little tingle of satisfaction from that to be honest. I guess talking shit to the audience isn't out of bounds. Which is sorta cool. That means as long as I'm not being a bitch to Ford or the crew, I can take all my frustration and fear out on the viewers.

Spencer comes back after a few more minutes and begins to paint a zipper on my new outfit. His paintbrush is minuscule, like that thing has two hairs attached to it, that's how thin it is. And Spencer knows just what to do with it. I watch as he loads it up with a silver paint, then he strokes it back and forth between my breasts.

He stops and dabs on more paint every now and then, but he's pretty efficient because that silver line down my front is looking like a zipper in about thirty minutes. He cleans the brush and adds some more color to his palette, then mixes it in with the silver, making a darker gray.

He dabs this color on, little pinpricks of dark in between the silver, and I'm so fascinated with his technique, watching him create a lifelike zipper from color, that I jump a little when Ford speaks next to me. "Wow, Spencer, I've seen the pictures, but I had no idea." Spencer is glaring at him because my little jump made him screw up. "Sorry," Ford says, looking at me apologetically.

Everyone is entranced by Spencer's skill and we all just stand there watching him paint for hours. After he finishes up the main zipper he paints on some zippered pockets. One on each breast, one on each hip, and then some zippers running down the side of my legs, from knee to ankle. He even adds glare to certain strategic places with a bright white color, making the entire outfit look like shiny latex instead of flat paint. When I look in the

MANIC

mirror I realize he's added a sharp collar around my neck, and he used solvent to remove some paint and make the outfit more revealing around my breasts. There are even realistic wrinkles in the zipper as it goes down my front.

The next time I look up at the clock it's after two and not only am I hungry and exhausted, but I have to pee as well. It took us almost eight hours to do this 'outfit'. I cannot imagine doing more than one in a day.

"OK," Spence says, swishing his brush in the paint cleaner. "We're ready for makeup. You need a restroom break, Rook?"

"Yes," I say emphatically.

"OK, no sitting down, squatting only and aim accurately. It won't come off easily, but be careful just the same, got it?"

I blush, but nod out a yes.

"Use the restrooms upstairs, then meet Josie in makeup."

"OK," I say, making my escape. I'm amazed at how not naked I feel. Team Rook follows me as I walk past all the crews and Ford like it's nothing. Then I bounce upstairs and fail to get even a second glance from anyone who happens to be working, not even Billy. He looks at me, lifts his head in a greeting and gives me a little wave.

He has no idea I'm naked.

I secretly grin as I make my way into the dressing room and find the bathrooms. Squatting isn't the easiest thing to do, especially when I'm all anxious about messing up Spencer's art, but it all works out. I almost forget and try to pull up my panties, then have to laugh at that.

Even *I* forgot I was naked.

I meet Josie in makeup and she oohs and ahhs at me so much everyone comes over to take a look. This time the fact that I'm naked is not lost on Billy and he grins. "Finally, I get to see Rook naked!"

"Shut up, Billy. Besides, if you remember, you groped my goods that first shoot we did."

"Oh yeah," he says thoughtfully. "Forgot about that. Sorry. I really didn't know you were that new, Rook, or I would've never been so aggressive."

Every girl in the makeup cubby groans and rolls her eyes, but I think it's cute that he apologized.

Hair and makeup is quick because I have Josie all to myself. She's now my personal makeup artist, no one else is allowed to use her until this contract is over. That means no leaving me sitting in the chair while she goes to attend to something else.

She pulls my hair back so tight I almost look bald when she's done. She leaves the ends in a long ponytail and then goes to work on my face. Mostly it's just your basic toner stuff and some bitchin' long eyelashes. I can barely see past them, they're so long.

She tops me off with a dark plum lipstick then adds some shine to it.

And I'm ready for Antoine. When Josie spins me around he's standing just outside Elise's salon, smiling. "You look beautiful, Rook, should we send Ronin a picture?"

I nod, embarrassed at his compliment. He's never said anything about how I look before, which sounds funny since that's pretty much the only thing he's concerned about around here—how we all look through the lens of his camera. It's almost like he's got a sort of professional detachment from us girls.

I like it.

But I also like his compliment, because he'd never say that to me unless it was true.

He takes my hand when I approach and leads me over to the bike under the afternoon light shining through the massive two-story windows. There's a bunch of studio lights as well, and about ten people to help him get what he needs. But I ignore all that. He lets go of my hand when we reach the bike and then asks me softly in a mixture of French and English that I only half understand to do things.

And the shoot begins.

NINE

ROOK

At first it's just Antoine telling me what to do, but everyone else is there as well. Since Spencer plays many roles in this contract, he's not only the artist, but the director of the catalog photo shoots, and it doesn't take long to figure out he and Antoine have very different visions about what these shots should look like.

Antoine is not happy about this and I can see his point. People usually hire him for his artistic interpretation. But Spencer is an artist too, so there's a whole lot of polite disagreement going on.

"Hey," I interrupt Spencer telling Antoine how he wants my body to hug the line of the seat and the tank. "Spencer, I think you should take five. Let Antoine do his job. Because I'm really tired here, and you guys just wasted like forty-five minutes with this bullshit vision stuff."

Ford snuffs out a laugh in the corner.

I might have stepped over the line. "I mean," I say, walking up to Spencer and putting on a pouty face, "he's famous, Spencer. His talent is the whole reason you guys chose Chaput Studios, right?"

Spencer shrugs.

"Just let him do it his way today, it's just one bike. We've got plenty more for you guys to make adjustments."

"Yeah, OK, but make sure you get the details of her body, Antoine, don't hide the sexy parts, man. We want guys zooming in on her, ya know? We want them to zoom in for tits and see the details on the gas tank, or the chrome on the tailpipe when they look at her legs."

Antoine responds angrily in French but Billy is the only one who appears to understands what he's saying, and he throws his hands up and says, "Leave me out of it."

But whatever Antoine said, Spencer walks out and Antoine refuses to speak English after that. He uses Billy and this time Billy does get involved, because even I know the French word for dollars.

"OK, Rook," Billy says after Antoine whispers something and then starts messing with his camera crap. "Sit on the seat backwards, then lie back on the tank." I do what he says and this makes my back arch and my tits stick way up. "Now turn your upper body slightly, so we get the"—Antoine says something here—"tank shot."

Right, I sneer to myself. *The tank shot.* It's got nothing to do with my nipples.

I just stop thinking and do what I'm told—that *is* the secret to being a good model. Billy moves me around like a mannequin, Antoine stays in French, and Spencer never comes back. Team Rook keeps far back from Antoine, maybe guessing he's about to morph into super-asshole at any moment over this shoot, and Ford, to his credit, says absolutely nothing. He just sits in a director's chair far off to the side, almost in another set, in fact.

Antoine finishes up pretty quick and I'm not sure if that's a good thing or a bad thing, but either way, Spencer returns, like he was standing outside the studio door just waiting for it to be over, and walks up to me. "Come with me, Rook, I'll wash the paint off you and then we're all going out to dinner."

I do not want to go out to dinner, but I'm too tired to argue at the moment. He puts his hand on the small of my back and leads me back down to the third floor, but this time we don't go back to the art room, we go through a set of double doors at the end of the hallway.

It's a shower room and there's already a bucket and a large sponge waiting next to one of the shower stations.

He turns the water on and waves over to the stream coming down from the shower head. "Rinse off and then I'll scrub you down with this paint remover. Sorry it's so personal, but it was either me or Billy and Antoine said me. So…"

He looks guilty.

"Doesn't anyone ever ask me about these things? I mean, maybe I can, you know, shower all by myself?"

He sighs. "You can't reach the back, Rook." He points to the bucket. "That's the paint thinner we use for this special body paint. It needs to be scrubbed."

I go stand under the shower and wet myself down and Spencer enters the room with me, staying out of the water blast as best as he can, and begins to scrub the paint off. It runs down my body in long ribbons of inky black streams.

"All that work, gone. It's sorta sad, huh, Spence?" I look over my shoulder at him and he's smiling.

"Yeah, this part sucks, but that's why we have Antoine. You were right earlier, I should butt out. I know this is hard work for you, believe me, I understand how hard models actually work. So I'm grateful you were so patient today and you did real well, for it being your first time."

"It wasn't bad. I think the outfit helped, you were right, I never felt naked." But now that the paint is being stripped away and there's no black buffer between Spencer's wandering eyes and my body, it does make me squirm a bit.

"And just so you know," Spencer says, interrupting my thoughts, "I'm not taking advantage of you, OK? It's just that we get one chance to capture this artwork, ya know?"

"Yeah, I know. Wait, who said you were taking advantage of me?"

"Antoine, that's what he said when he was speaking French back there because I want all your sexy parts in the photos and he was going out of his way to cover those bits up. It's just, I get it, he's making *art*. But I'm selling bikes to horny guys, so I need those shots, Rook. I'm not trying to take advantage."

Now that my back has been scrubbed clean, he bends down to scrub my butt and the back of my legs. I turn around and look at him because, yeah, that's a bit personal.

Spencer ignores me, either he doesn't care that it's personal, or he's trying to pretend it's not. The sponge is rubbing all over my ass when it dips between my legs a little making me gasp.

Spencer stands up. "OK, you can do the rest." He plops the sponge down in the bucket and walks out of the shower room, leaving me there to manage on my own.

These people get more and more confusing with every job. How am I supposed to process this? Spencer gets to paint me up then wash me down. All of me, my entire body. He gets to touch my ass and put his brush between my breasts. And Billy gets to manipulate my body into weird contortions so my nipples are standing at attention in every shot, even for the fucking fender— that was some feat, but that Billy is resourceful—and Antoine gets to take pictures of all this, while Ford and the crew stand around and record every facial expression on each of us as we do these things and try to remain professional.

I'm pretty sure my relationship with Ronin is over. Because no man, I don't care what kind of Catholic saint he is, would ever put up with this arrangement. Elise was right, I'm paying the price for this STURGIS contract, and I'm paying up front, because this is day fucking one and I have to do this shit all summer long.

I pick up the sponge, soak it with the remover solution, and scrub as fast as I can. All I want is to go back up to Ronin's apartment and take a real shower, but I can't do that until the paint's all gone. And Ford can go fuck himself, because I need that shower. It's not a luxury or a way to hide, my shower just isn't adequate enough to deal with the amount of cleaning my body will require at the end of these shoots.

Luckily Spencer left me a nice soft towel, so I wrap myself up in that and head back to the studio to make a break for the Beast. No one is around when I slip in, so I tiptoe as best as I can with my wet feet, and head upstairs. As soon as I turn the corner towards Ronin's apartment, I see Ford.

He wags his finger at me and smiles. "I knew already, Rook. Nice try, but the crew is waiting on the terrace, go shower in your own place."

I punch in Ronin's code as I ignore him.

"You can do this, I can't stop you, but I *will* fine you, Rook. The deal is that you live at your apartment, not here."

I sigh and run through my options. Ford is a control guy, even if I was wrong about Ronin, I know for a fact I'm not wrong about Ford. He thinks he's Mister Dominant. I turn around and smile at him. "Ford, I swear, I'll shower in my own place on days that have no body paint, OK? It's just my shower isn't really a shower, it's a claw-foot tub with this pathetic sprayer system and I can't…" I stop to pout and open my eyes a little wider as I stare up at his face. "I just can't relax in that thing. And now that I have all this crap on my body, I can't even get clean in it!"

I'm not sure what I expected, I don't know him that well, but "Nice try, sweet cheeks," definitely wasn't it.

"Fine, I'll pay you to use the shower, bill me for it."

"People watch reality shows because they think they'll get to see something personal, the whole shower setup is part of that. It's a big part of that, in fact."

"How much?"

"How much what?"

"How much do you want to let me take showers at Ronin's place? Just give me a number."

MANIC

Ford actually covers his mouth with his hand to hide his smile. "You're trying to pay me off?"

"Just tell me how much the fine is, asshole. This job will probably ruin my life, so I'll be damned if I'm gonna spend one more second worrying about getting a decent fucking shower."

"OK, would you like to make a deal, Rook? How about you go to breakfast with me tomorrow morning. Five AM. If you do that, I'll look past the shower this time. But only this time."

"Breakfast? You want to buy me breakfast?"

He shrugs like he's playing innocent, but he's got a devious gleam in his eye.

"Whatever." I push the door open and then quickly close it behind me.

I wash off the paint thinner in the Beast, and I tell you what, I'd have breakfast, lunch, and dinner with Ford to keep using this thing. I figured out how to make the steam come out from the ceiling and it makes the whole experience feel like a tropical island. It's only after I'm all done that I realize I have no clothes.

I don't keep clothes at Ronin's place because that would imply that our relationship was more than just dating, and now I regret that. I search through his closet—which is spectacular—and find a pair of old jeans and a dark green t-shirt. The pants are way too loose, but there's plenty of belts, so I grab one of those too. I have no bra, but I can change just as soon as I get back to my place.

Dinner is not something I'm really up for but they are all waiting for me down in front of Antoine's office. I try to sneak by, but Team Rook is waiting just off to the side of the stairs, like they were trying to ambush me. I hustle out to the terrace, they follow, but I smile in satisfaction when I go inside my apartment and they have to wait outside. I grab some clothes and then pull on some shorts and a tank top and complete my outfit with my old Converse sneakers. I don't care how many pairs of expensive shoes I get, nothing beats a well-worn pair of Converse.

When I go back out the crew follows me again. I huff out an annoyed breath, but they ignore me like a good crew.

"Rook!" Antoine barks as I enter the studio again. "Good, we're starving. I sent Ronin a picture, he said he's tried calling you, but you never pick up."

"Oh, duh. I don't have my phone on me. I'm not used to carrying it around in here."

"You can call later."

"How's everything, did he say?"

Antoine gets a worried look on his face as Ford and Spencer join us and we walk down the stairs. "Clare is OK, Ronin is the only one she's ever listened to, she's always been difficult. I'm just glad he's there."

"Yeah, I'm glad too," I say, but I catch Ford's smug look out of the corner of my eye.

We walk over to Cookie's then take our booth in back like normal. Antoine scoots in and then Spencer takes the seat next to him, so I'm stuck near the window with Ford on the other side of me. The waitress, not one that I recognize, brings us drinks and I order the Big Breakfast Special instead of dinner. Antoine and Spencer get the diner version of steaks, and Ford orders an egg-white omelet.

I sigh as we sit. I'm tired of these guys already and it's the first day, but I do notice one thing. "Hey, where's our camera crews?"

Ford points up to the ceiling. "We paid Cookie's to let us tap into their security cameras and we have a microphone hidden nearby. So as long as you come in here, no crew will follow."

"Good to know," I say dryly. "Anywhere without a camera crew is good."

"OK, I'm just going to go ahead and ask, Rook. Because I don't understand. Why the hell did you take this contract if you didn't want to be on camera?"

I look over at Spencer and he's wincing, but Antoine's the one who answers. "Spencer left that part out when he explained the terms to her. She didn't know, Ford."

"Hey, I never thought she'd take the contract that night. Rook, tell them, you were a little impulsive, remember?"

"I was," I admit. "It's not Spencer's fault. Ronin and I were fighting and I overreacted and signed the contract without talking it over first."

Ford just looks at me but says nothing. The three of them talk about bikes and photo shoots, and even old times, since Antoine has known both Ford and Spencer since they were in high school. I don't participate much and I'm just too tired to think about making meaningless conversation.

After we eat Antoine and Spencer head over to a sports bar to watch the Rockies play the Padres in San Diego and Ford and I walk back to the studio in silence. I punch in my code when we get to the doors and then stop and turn to him when he tries to follow me in. "Aren't you going home?"

"I need to check on Larry's crew before the day's over." He holds the door open wider and beckons me to enter. We walk up the stairs in silence again, then he heads off at the third floor, waving a gesture back at me which might pass as a goodbye.

I continue up to the fourth floor and then make my way out onto the terrace. It's a beautiful night and since it's Monday, it's also quiet. I go inside my garden apartment and grab my cell phone. Sure enough, there are seven missed calls from Ronin. I press redial and walk back outside to sit on the grass under the cherry trees.

He never picks up, of course. He's probably mad at me for forgetting my phone, or maybe he took one look at that photo Antoine sent him of me in the painted-up latex suit and decided Clare the junkie was a much better fit for him.

Being jealous sucks. I hate it. I hate the feeling you get when all you want is to hear your boyfriend's voice on the other end of a phone. It's a horrible feeling and I don't even understand how something as little as getting someone's voicemail can ruin a perfectly fine day. And this day wasn't so bad, really. I mean, it was better than the first day I was groped by Billy. That was a weird day. I lie back on the grass and look up at the canopy of leaves on the cherry trees and then close my eyes for a second.

"Rook?"

"Huh?" I sit up, confused. "What?"

Ford is kneeling down next to me. "Why are you sleeping outside?"

"I just dozed off, Ford. Shit, cut me a break, will ya?

"Are you sure that's all it was?"

"What else would it be?"

"Not wanting to sleep inside under the cameras."

I laugh and sigh at the same time. "Yeah, forgot about them, thanks for reminding me though. I appreciate that."

"Well, if you prefer to sleep under the cherry trees let me know, I'll put some cameras up there too."

I glare at him. "You probably would, too." I get up and brush off my shorts. "Well, I'm heading in."

"We're still on for breakfast tomorrow?"

I snort out a laugh this time. "Yeah, we're on."

"Wear something comfortable," he calls out as I walk away. I leave him there and make my way inside, not even bothering to turn the lights on. I just sleepwalk back to my bed and crash, not even remembering to squish myself into the corner or wear pants to bed so the audience can't get a good look at my ass in the morning.

TEN

ROOK

Why, God? Just why? Why do people insist on pounding on my door at the most ungodly hours? "I'm coming!" I scream. The pounding stops and I reach for my phone. It's five after five in the morning.

What the fuck?

I roll out of bed and stumble down the hall, then throw the door open and shield my eyes from the morning sun.

"You're not ready." Ford frowns down at me.

I look down at my shorts, then up at him, and shoot him my own frown. "Give me a second." I leave the door open and shuffle back to the bedroom, grab a clean pair of shorts and a tank top—

"I said comfortable and loose, but you'll need a good bra."

"What?" I shake my head at Ford, who is peeking his head around the corner of my closet.

I look down at his clothes and recognize the garb of trendy exercisers the world over. His outfit looks like he pulled it off the rack at Sports Authority this morning. "Ford, you said breakfast.

MANIC

I do not work out."

"It is breakfast, you'll see. Unless you want to take showers in that claw-foot monstrosity down the hall?"

"All right, get out. I'll meet you outside."

He backs off and I grab some sporty stuff that Ronin gave me from the Chaput closet when I first got here. The tank top has a built-in bra and it's a pretty coral color. The sport shorts are black with a matching coral racing stripe going up the sides of my thighs. I look the part until I put on my shoes, and that makes me laugh because all I have for my feet in the way of sneakers are my Converse.

I brush my teeth and pull my hair back in a ponytail, then head outside. Ford is talking with Team Rook over by the picnic tables. I guess that means we're not going to Cookie's, since the crew isn't necessary for that eatery.

"Ready?" Ford asks as I approach. "Nice shoes," he says, shaking his head.

"What are we doing?"

"You'll see, just follow."

I do what I'm told—I'm used to that anyway—and we walk down the stairs and go outside using the back door that leads out into the parking lot, then cross Blake Street and we're at Coors Field, the baseball stadium where the Rockies play. Ronin loves baseball and we've gone to two games together already. "We're eating breakfast at the stadium?"

"Yes, afterward, anyway."

"After what?"

He never answers, just walks us around the side and stops at a plain gray metal door that has no windows at all. He knocks and it opens immediately. The Mexican guy on the other side greets Ford in Spanish and they act like old friends, laughing and joking and shaking hands. He finally turns to us. "Rook, this is Jose, he's the head guy back here. I've known him since I was a kid. I used to come to the stadium every morning until I graduated from college a few years ago." Then he looks over at

Team Rook and says, "Sorry, guys, only one guest allowed."

I smile at that and follow Ford into the dark hallway. So whatever we're doing here, we're doing it in private. I'll take any privacy I can get at this point. I follow him through the convoluted hallways until he pushes through a door and we come out on a stairwell. "Which way, Rook? Up or down?"

"What are you up to?"

"Just pick, up or down."

"Down," I say, "because climbing stairs is not my idea of fun right now."

He stifles a chuckle and leads the way down the stairs, then we get to another landing and he pushes through a set of double doors and we're in the stands, about midway up.

"Cool," I say, still not sure what the hell is going on. He walks over to the railing and looks out. I follow of course. There are a few other people here, all running up and down the stairs spread out across the seats across from us. "I sincerely hope"—I stop to snort here—"that you do not expect me to *run*, Ford. Especially up and down stairs. Because I'm not a runner. I'm a slow walker at best, possibly a shuffler, or an aimless wanderer, but never a runner."

He's just smiling.

"I'm serious."

"I can tell, but so am I. So I'll make you a deal, OK? You run stadiums with me every morning and I'll let you shower at Ronin's any time you want. As long"—he stops to give me a stern look—"as you don't take advantage and start spending all your free time in the shower."

"Why?"

"Why what?"

"Why do you want me to run these steps with you? There's a reason, you're just not telling me, so maybe I'll agree, but I wanna know the real reason you want me to do this with you. Are you coming on to me? Trying to piss off Ronin? What?"

His smile falters for half a moment, then it's back, brighter

MANIC

than ever. "Are you sure you want the real reason? Because most people prefer white lies to truth."

I roll my eyes. "Just tell me. There's no need for drama, Ford."

"Fine." He shrugs. "I want you to run with me in the morning because you're too young to take this job and maybe I don't know your whole story, but I'm perceptive enough to see that there's something *wrong* with you. I'm not sure what it is, I don't even want to know what it is, but this job will change your life. So instead of letting you dwell on how much it sucks and how big a mistake you really made when you took this contract, or beating the shit out of Spencer for letting you, or belittling Ronin for not being able to control you better—I'm just gonna take it upon myself to save you." He stops to pan his arms wide at the empty stadium. "With exercise. Because it will help, take my word on that."

"That is the dumbest shit I've ever heard."

He busts out a laugh. "You're a fighter, that's for sure. And I'm not gonna ask, Rook, so don't wait for that moment. I do not care why you come off as broken, I really don't. I'm just not gonna be the guy responsible for making it worse."

"Well, I'm not gonna exert myself, Ford. I'll *walk* up the stairs."

He turns his back and starts running up the steps. "Fine with me, just don't stop climbing until I do. That's the deal."

I huff out some air and drag my feet up the steps. When I look up to see where he is, he's already finished this set and is running down the middle landing to the next set. He descends those stairs with just as much enthusiasm. I trudge my way up to the landing, then find him again. That asshole is like four sets of stairs away from me now.

It's like reverse psychology or something, right? He thinks he can shame me into putting in more effort, but he's wrong. I'm naturally lazy when it comes to athletic pursuits. I like sitting in the stands at the baseball game, not playing. Or running stadiums, for God's sake. I reach the bottom of my second set and then walk over to the next one. When I look up to find Ford, he's like a million miles away now.

We do this for a good while before I notice him starting to make his way back towards me. My legs are a little sore, but I do exactly what I said I would. I practically mope up these steps. I only cover a few aisles, that's how much I mope, but Ford, he does almost half the stadium, *at a fucking run*, before he turns back towards me.

I wait for him on the landing as he bursts up the last set of stairs and then stops to breathe hard, bending over a little in the process.

Damn, the guy really made an effort, he's dripping sweat, and I'm still fresh as can be. Not even thirsty. "I thought you said we were gonna eat, Ford?" He laughs, but he's still very much out of breath. "Shit, dude, you really take this stuff seriously, don't you?"

"Feels good, Rook. It feels good to run it off every morning."

"No," I say, shaking my head. "Mornings are for sleeping in and eating breakfast. Speaking of which, I'm starving, where's my food?"

He waves a hand at me to enter the stadium doors, not the way we came, but the way you go to get snacks during a game. We both go inside and Ford whips his shirt off and starts dabbing it across his wet body.

I steal a look. I'm a girl, I can't help it, he's not bad-looking. His hair is lighter than Ronin's, but not blondish like Spencer's. He's got a bit of scruff on his chin left over from yesterday. But I bet he shaves it when he gets home because he's more of a clean-cut kinda guy. The complete opposite of Spencer, who is one hundred percent biker, and Ronin, who comes off as hip and edgy.

Ford's look says *goal-oriented* or *I come from a long line of bankers*. I tuck down a laugh at those thoughts and sneak a look at his body. It's very nice. Maybe not Top Model Ronin nice, but still nice. He obviously takes very good care of himself.

MANIC

He catches me looking and smiles as I turn away quickly.

We walk along the interior corridor for a while and the smell of breakfast food wafts into my nose. "Food!"

"They keep a stand open for us in the morning. Breakfast burritos."

"So, let me get this straight, you bust your ass to burn calories, then come eat breakfast burritos? That makes no sense."

"We're not here to lose weight, Rook. People who have access to the stadium are training, which means we eat a lot of food when we're done."

"What are you training for?" I can't help myself, he's made me curious with his secret endorphin-rush addiction.

"Life, just like you," is all he says before we come to the counter and he's ordering us food and orange juice. He pays, then we walk back outside and find seats in the empty stands.

The burrito is good and even though I didn't expend much energy, I do feel awake and have more pep than I usually do in the morning. I better be careful or that reverse psychology shit will start working on me and before you know it, I might turn into one of those annoying freaks who thinks all manner of physical activity is *fun*.

We don't say much after that. Just eat. Then he takes my trash and throws it away and we walk back over to the studio building and part ways. He goes to his car and I walk upstairs, grab some clothes to stash at Ronin's, then head up to his place and enjoy my totally legal kick-ass shower.

Smiling.

ELEVEN

ROOK

Team Rook was nowhere to be found when I made my way to Ronin's apartment door, but when I emerge freshly showered, they are waiting outside in the hallway. We all act like I'm the only person there and all I hear is the scuffle of their shoes as they follow me downstairs to the third floor art room.

Spencer is already rocking out to that Bad to the Bone song, singing along quite loud for a guy, and messing around with some paints and brushes. "Yo, Rookie! I'm glad you came back for day two. Sometimes the girls skip out after the first session, but I guess I played it cool, because here you are!"

"I signed a contract, Spencer. I can't skip out. And please, do not ever call me Rookie again. I will go apeshit on you."

"Noted. But I played it cool, right? That's the real reason you came back, right?"

"Right," I say, smiling. It's hard not to enjoy being around Spencer. He's a clown, and a hot one at that. He's got on his usual garb today, a Shrike Bikes t-shirt, old faded Levis, and biker

MANIC

boots. Even though I've seen him like a bazillion times, I've never seen him wear the same t-shirt twice. And they are cool designs, not your typical black and orange Harley eagles or big-titted girls with American flag bandannas wrapped around their heads screen-printed on those cheap-ass black polyester shirts.

The designs on Spencer's shirts look like someone drew them with a charcoal pencil. This one is a light gray and has a blackbird on it, beak open like it's cawing, bending down with wings half open, like it's about to take flight. It says *Shrike Raven* in big bold letters on top, and at the bottom it has the new Shrike motto, *Not Your Daddy's Ride.*

I know that's a dig at Spencer's father because Ronin told me. He retired a few years back and left the business to Spencer, and Spencer, wanting to make his own name, came up with that tag line to let everyone know this was his game now.

And he's done pretty well. The guy's not even twenty-five and he's taken the company from small pop-and-son to mega-commercial in like two years.

Spence notices my gaze and points down to the raven on his chest. "This is one of the designs we're gonna use to promote the bike, but I'm gonna make one of you too."

"You're part of the merchandising package, Rook." For the first time I notice Ford sitting in the corner in that director's chair. "I just thought I'd let you know that, in case Spencer conveniently forgot to mention your face will be made into dolls and put on clothing." He says it in an irritated voice and then Spencer flips him off and turns away, busying himself with his art supplies again.

"Wonderful," I say to no one in particular. "How lucky am I? Don't all girls want to be turned into Barbie?"

"Yeah," Ford says, again with the irritation, "but I'm pretty sure Biker Barbie was never part of your girlhood fantasy, was it?"

I scowl at him. "What's your deal, Ford? I'm a big girl, OK? I'm fine with the doll shit. It's a fucking doll. Who cares, they'll probably make like five hundred of them, people will buy them, break them, lose them, destroy them—whatever—and it will be over. It's not like someone's naming a fucking battleship after me."

Ford says nothing, just keeps his bad mood to himself over in the corner.

"OK, well, what's the plan today, Spence?"

"Bikinis, four of them."

I shake my head trying to imagine four paintings and photo shoots. 'That sounds like a long day."

"Well"—Ford is back in action again—"it's not really, Rook. Because the term bikini is used loosely here." I mouth the words *shut up* at him, but he looks right at me and continues talking. "Because those little postage stamps Spencer is going to paint over your nipples barely count as clothing, or paint for that matter."

Spencer turns around, his eyes blazing, his whole demeanor screaming *fuck you*. "That's it, Ford, I warned you. Out. I'm not putting up with your bullshit."

For a second I figure this is some theatrics for the sake of the cameras, but when I look over at Team Spencer, they start to get uncomfortable. Team Rook steps back, like these two are about to throw. "OK, what's going on? Are you guys fighting? I mean, I just saw you an hour ago, Ford. What's the problem?"

"The problem is what Spencer plans to do with you today, even though Antoine told him there's no one to help you between shoots, that's the problem."

"Spencer?" I ask, totally lost.

Ford continues, not even giving Spencer a chance to talk. "Well, let's walk through this, Rook. Spencer's gonna paint you up in a bikini, but he wants to do four shoots today, so that means that paint will have to be washed off four times." He stops to stare at me. "I think you can put two and two together from there."

"So Spencer will have to wash me off? Is this the problem?"

I look over at Spencer and he shrugs. "Rook, I gotta get through this catalog and get back up to Fort Collins by Friday, so

MANIC

we have to get as many shoots as we can. The bikinis are popular, easy, and quick."

"Hey, I could care less, Spencer. I'm not sure what Ford's problem is, but I'm pretty sure you're not painting on bikinis to feel me up." I roll my eyes. "Let's just do this."

Ford actually gets up and walks out.

I look back over at Spencer and he throws up his hands and turns back to his supplies. "Just get naked, OK? Twist up your hair and we'll get started."

I take a deep breath and look over at the camera people, then say an internal *fuck it* and whip my shirt off right there. What's the point? They're gonna see me naked whether I strip in that pathetic excuse of a dressing room or right here in front of them. I watch them as I do it too, daring them to even snicker. My look keeps them professional and when I glance back at Spencer he's laughing at me.

"You are something else, I swear. OK, first up is the *white bikini*." He says this last part loud, like he wants Ford, who is all the way across the room talking to Director Larry, to hear him. "White, so we can *paint over it*," he yells. "And not have to *wash it off*."

Spencer and I do a collective eye roll and try not to laugh.

"OK, Rook, just come stand here in the middle of the sheet." Spencer checks for Ford and drops his voice to a whisper and winks at me. "It might get a bit personal, but just know, I'm a licensed professional, Rook."

"Where have I heard that before? Oh, yeah, Ronin, when he was teaching me to shampoo his hair."

Spencer gives me a stupid look and I shrug. "Never mind."

Spencer's got his paints and brushes all laid out on a rolling cart this time. He catches me eyeing them and explains. "No airbrush today, right? It's all detail. So it goes a little slower at first, but the bikinis are so small, it won't be bad this time."

"This time?"

"Yeah, well," he says, kneeling down in front of me. "The other outfits aren't so easy. I've got something spectacular planned for Sturgis, that job will take all day, in fact we'll probably have to get up in the middle of the night in order to have it ready for the public presentation, which is later in the afternoon."

I think about this for a minute, trying to picture what that last shoot will be like, but even though I've seen all sorts of pictures of Sturgis, I've never been there before. And even though yesterday was pretty long, I can't imagine what it might take for Spencer to actually paint me all night long and into the morning.

His paintbrush on my lower stomach snaps me out of my daydreaming and I gasp as he drags it across my skin. His face is like right *there*. He's practically breathing on my sensitive little button!

"Sorry," he says, looking up at me. "There's just no good place to start this project. It's here, your ass, or your tits. Might as well get the hard part out of the way, right?"

I say nothing. Because honestly, I really didn't think this through.

I twist my head a little and find Antoine off to the side, his hand over his mouth trying to hide a frown. "Hey, Antoine. What's up?"

He stays right where he is, which is really too far away to have a normal conversation. "Ronin called. He can't reach you, he said. He wants you to call him right away."

I look down at Spencer but he's practically got his head buried in my girly parts, and if he cares that Ronin wants me to call him, he doesn't show it. I shrug a little, which makes Spencer grunt at me to stand still. "Can you dial the phone and hand it to me?" I'm secretly dying to talk to Ronin, it's been days and even though I was the one who said things should stay casual, I miss him. Like bad.

Antoine shakes his head. "No, not now. After we finish the first shoot, I'll call him back and tell him." And then Antoine walks out.

"Well," Ford says, from behind me. "Here we go."

MANIC

"What's that mean?"

"Ignore that dickhead," Spence says, clearly irritated. "He's just jealous."

"Rook," Ford says, grabbing a chair and positioning himself off to the side, just out of my peripheral vision. "You do realize as soon as Ronin sees what's going on here, he's gonna be pissed? You do realize this, right?"

"Are you trying to make me feel bad on purpose?"

"Ford," Spencer growls, "I fucking told you to get the fuck out of here. No more talking to Rook, follow your own goddamn rules for once, will ya? She's just doing her job and if Ronin has a problem with it, he can take it up with me."

"Why would Ronin have a problem with it? It's not a secret." I don't get this weirdness going on with Ford and Spencer. "He's OK with the job, Ford, we talked about it."

"Did you talk about having Spencer between your legs drawing bikini bottoms?"

Spencer rushes Ford and they both crash through the flimsy partition pretending to be a dressing room. Spencer throws a punch that lands squarely on Ford's jaw, and a split second later Ford is back up on his feet and he pounces on Spencer. They grapple on the floor, landing punches and doing weird shit with their legs, trying to get the upper hand. All the crew on the other side of the room and Team Spencer start pulling them apart. Team Rook keeps filming.

They both stand there, breathing heavy, red-faced and lips bleeding. "Out!" Spencer growls. I've never pictured Spencer mad before, but right now he's scaring the shit out of me. He looks like he might kill Ford.

When I look over to Ford, he's the complete opposite, his tie a little crooked, but generally, he looks calm. Spencer's anger barely touches him.

I think I have a new respect for Ford.

Antoine and his team enter just then and he is roaring, not really in French or English, but a strange mixture of both. He's talking to Spencer and the only word I really catch is *stop*.

I look over to my team and they look just as scared as I feel.

This studio has one rule. Just one. And that rule involves the word stop.

"Are we done for today?" I ask Antoine.

"Yes. Put your clothes on, go home, and call Ronin. *Now*."

I do as I'm told. Fuck these guys. I don't know why every single fucking time the men around here get in a fight everyone always acts like it's my fucking fault. I stomp away like a baby, my team doggedly following, then leave them all outside when I go back inside my apartment. My phone is still on the night table next to my bed, and when I wake it up I have seventeen missed calls.

No voicemails.

I press redial for Ronin's phone and he answers on the first ring.

"Shit, Gidget, it's about time!"

"Sorry, I keep forgetting to keep it on me. You're never gonna believe what just happened!"

"Let me guess, Ford and Spencer?"

"Yeah, how'd you know?"

"We have history, that's all. I don't even know why Spencer took this gig, he knows Ford will just piss him off."

"Antoine called stop, so I guess we're done for today."

"Well," he laughs. "That's a first. What'd they do? Get in a brawl?"

"Yes, Spencer charged him like he was Juggernaut. He kinda scared me, Ronin."

Ronin breathes out slowly on the other end and I can't really tell if he's frustrated with me, or just trying to remain calm. "He'd never hurt you, Rook, OK? He never would."

"Well, I just want this contract to be over. Can't you call Antoine and tell him to let Spencer finish these outfits today?"

I can hear Elise talking in the background, then a muffled noise, like Ronin's covering up the phone. "Yeah, OK. I'll have

MANIC

Elise call him. We won't be home until Sunday, Gidge, so just hang tight, OK? Clare's not doing well, she needs us right now. She really needs Antoine, to be honest, but he's got the contract. It's just really fucked up."

Sunday? I privately pout, then immediately feel guilty because Clare is physically sick trying to get over her addiction and I'm just caught up in my own stupid decisions. "Don't worry about me, OK? She's way more important than this job."

There's a loud knock on the door and I peek down the hallways to see who's there. "Ford's at my door, I guess I better go."

"All right, Rook, call me before you go to bed, OK? Antoine said he's taking you to dinner tonight, so don't let Ford or Spencer talk you into anything."

"OK."

"I miss you real bad, ya know that, right?"

I smile into the phone as Ford's knocking becomes pounding. "I miss you a lot, too. I really do."

"See ya Sunday. Love you."

I sit there, my mouth hanging open, wondering if I'm supposed to say it back. But before I can decide, I hear the line click off. He didn't wait to find out.

I let out a long breath.

Then smile.

I'll be ready next time.

TWELVE

ROOK

"What can I do for you, Ford?"

He runs his hand through his hair and grimaces. "I'd just like to apologize, I was out of line. I'll keep my mouth shut from now on. Antoine has revoked the stop order. We can proceed."

Well, that's not what I was expecting, but nonetheless, just looking at him is pissing me off. "You know what, Ford? I don't really care why all you guys hate each other, I really don't. But I'm just trying to make a living. This is a job, Ford. A job I actually need, or else I wouldn't be doing it. So if you assholes can't control yourself, just don't hang around, OK? Because the next time you guys fight in front of me, I'm calling a lawyer to see how difficult I can make your life, you got it? Maybe it's too late to quit, but I promise you, I'll make you regret you ever met me if you try this shit again. I'm not interested in your big-brother routine, I have a boyfriend, I'm not looking for your brand of friendship, so butt the fuck out!"

MANIC

He just nods as I walk past and hurry across the terrace, trying not to smile at Team Rook as they hide their chuckles, and then hoof it back down to the art room.

Ford does not follow.

Antoine is still half-yelling at Spencer, in French, so apparently he understands him, and Spencer's expression is a cross between irritated, angry, and embarrassed.

I clear my throat when I reach them and Antoine turns around.

"Spencer, I'm gonna tell you the same thing I told Ford. If you pull this shit in front of me again, I'll make you sorry. I'll hire lawyers, I'll ruin this show, I'll be the worst model you can imagine." I drop the robe and stand there as Antoine turns away and walks out. "Now, paint the fucking bikinis. Do not breathe on any sensitive areas. Do not even talk to me right now because I'm pissed. We just wasted a whole bunch of time, and I'm ready to get the fuck back to work."

He shrinks back a little as my words get sharper, but then nods and goes over to his supplies and starts getting it together again. I look back at my team and wink and then catch Producer Larry and his people on the other side of the room snickering.

A few minutes later Spencer is back kneeling on the floor in front of me, painting furiously fast, not being all that careful if you ask me, and not saying one word.

And that's OK with me.

I stand still, I turn, I kneel, I even lie down and spread my fucking legs at one point, but I could care less.

This outfit is boring compared to the last one, but Ford was right about one thing, there's not a lot of paint involved.

Today when I go back upstairs for the first photo shoot I absolutely feel naked. My nipples are white stars that have bikini strings attached to them. It looks real enough, Spencer did his magic and painted wrinkles in the fabric and shaded it just right so it tricks you into believing the illusion, but I don't feel dressed and I don't feel sexy.

76

Josie bundles up my hair in something that looks like an old-ass bathing cap and then slaps on a blonde wig cut into a flirty bob with straight bangs. She brushes my cheeks with bronzer and a little bit of pink to give the illusion of a slight sunburn after a day in the sun, then drags some mascara through my lashes. It's all very natural, except for the wig.

Billy has materialized from somewhere and to be honest, I'm happy about that. Billy and I got off on the wrong foot, but he's very professional and after spending time with Ford and Spencer, I can appreciate the tight ship that Antoine normally runs here. I miss Elise's watchful eyes and Ronin's calming gestures. These guys would've never pulled this shit if Ronin and Elise were here.

Billy doesn't make one crack about me being naked this time and I'm not sure if Antoine warned him to keep his mouth shut or if he's just smart enough to figure that out himself, but either way, he makes me feel better. "Ready, Rook?" he asks in a low voice.

"Yeah, I'm good." I go over to the bike we're shooting today. It's an old-school soft-tail that sorta reminds me of those classic Fifties cars, with the white walled tires and the off-white colored frame. The gas tank really sets it off because it's fat and has a pretty powder-blue Shrike logo on it, which is never the same thing twice. Each custom bike gets its own custom logo to match. This one is a spiked skull and crossbones, but painted up with fancy lines and swirls. It's kinda girly.

I almost wish I had chosen this bike as my ride, since Spencer promised to customize a bike for me from his showroom.

This bike only has one seat and it sits low. Billy tells me to cross my legs, then put them up on the handlebars. I sit sideways, then lean over and flash my ass, then back around to push out my tits. Even though Antoine's pictures will show a lot more skin in this shoot than they did yesterday, in my opinion it's not nearly as sexy as that catsuit.

"OK, Rook, that's enough." Antoine stops talking and looks behind him at Spencer. "She needs to wash this paint off?"

MANIC

Spencer looks uncomfortable. "No, I can paint over this one. Next time, though, yeah."

"Billy will take care of Rook in the shower until Ronin returns."

I smile all the way back down to the art room because these asshole men have been put in their place and Antoine must have really been pissed to tame Spencer like that. Ford never even came back up to the studio.

This next painting goes very quick because Spencer just adds to it, turning the stars into flowers and making the bottoms yellow and white stripes. I'm back up in the studio in less than an hour.

Josie just does touch-ups on my makeup and since I never took the wig off, the hair only needs a quick comb.

This time the bike is a sunny orange and it has a sandy floor and a beach backdrop behind it. Antoine has props for me now too, a wide-brimmed hat and a pair of orange sunglasses. Spencer appears after changing into some board shorts. He's got no shirt on and all his tattoos are now in plain sight. I guess I never paid much attention before, but all of Spencer's tattoos are red and black. I've never seen anything like it. It's clear that Spence plans his body art just as meticulously as he does his body painting.

Most of his tats are skulls and birds. And I guess this makes sense, a shrike is a little bird infamous for impaling insects on thorns. I looked his name up because it was so unusual. The birds on his arms and chest are not all shrikes, because those are little robin-sized birds. So despite their cool name and impressive impaling capabilities, they are not really suitable as the starring avian in Spencer's artwork.

No, most of his birds are large. I can see an eagle, an ibis, and lots and lots of ravens.

Or maybe they are rooks?

His front piece is the most beautiful blackbird tattoo I've ever seen and there are ribbons of red and smoky gray weaving around it, camouflaging skulls in the swirls. "Who does your art,

Spence? It's incredible."

He snorts out a laugh but doesn't answer, just takes my hand and leads me over to the bike.

"Oh, are you in this shot with me?" I ask, trying to sound nonchalant. I'm a little surprised because no one ever mentioned that Spencer and I would model together.

"Yeah, I'm the owner, right?'"

I squint at him. "Did you just pull rank on me?"

"Spencer," Antoine warns.

Spencer throws up his hands. "She asked me a question. Fuck! What am I supposed to do? Ignore her?" He takes a seat on the bike and then pats his lap. "Sit down here, Rook."

I hesitantly sit on his leg and he grunts. "Now look, Antoine, I'm paying for this fucking shoot, I need her to be natural, you've got her all wound up. Rook"—his attention goes back to me—"just pretend like you do in your other jobs. I'm your boyfriend, we're on sitting on the bike at the beach, and you *like* me."

I wrap my arms around his neck and scoot back on his lap a little more, which makes him suck in his breath—and makes me snicker a little if I'm honest—and then lean into his neck and whisper, "I do like you Spencer. But you scared me. I don't like that fighting stuff."

"I'm sorry," he says. "But I'm not taking advantage of you and I'm sick of everyone thinking I am."

Antoine is busy shooting as we talk and then he's barking out orders in French, which Spencer seems to understand.

"Do you speak French, too?"

"It's hard to know Antoine without learning French, he hates to speak English. And I took it in school so Ronin couldn't talk shit about me behind my back." He grins a devious smile down at me. "I know enough and Antoine says if I want good pictures I gotta get you to act like you're having a good time in my lap."

"Spencer!" Antoine barks.

Spence winks at me as he wraps me up in his arms. "I made that last part up, but it's true. Just give me some good pics, Rook.

MANIC

I saw the ones you did with Ronin and those were fucking hot."

I bite my lip a little. They are paying me a butt-load of money, a lot more than the TRAGIC contract was worth, so fuck it. If I'm gonna do this job, I might as well do it right. I lean in and kiss Spencer and Antoine's camera clicks like crazy. Spencer rubs my back a little and then he wraps his hands around my neck and pulls until we bump foreheads, our lips very close but not touching. I look down at him and smile.

"Thank you," he whispers.

"It's my job, right?"

"Right." He leans in and kisses me again. It feels... weird to do this and not have it be cheating. Is it cheating? I pull back and then Antoine tells me to stand on the other side of the bike and lean down on Spence's shoulders, draping my arms around his body.

The plus side to this pose is that it's not an ass-shot. But my tits are practically dangling right in front of Spencer's face. I try to pretend it's just a job, but the truth is, Spencer is excited, and while I am flattered to have that effect on him, I'm also kinda worried, because I'm a little turned on too.

Antoine asks for a few more poses, all of which compound the energy between us right now.

I do not like him that way, I tell myself emphatically.

That's not a lie either. I want Ronin.

But there is a purely physical part of me that can't help but respond.

When Antoine finally gets what he needs I get up quickly and trot downstairs to wash this paint off. Billy dutifully follows me.

"So," he says, grinning, as I turn on the water and grab the sponge that is already in the bucket of paint cleaner on the floor of the shower room. "It's not as easy as it looks, is it?"

"What's not?"

"Keeping it professional."

"Did it show?"

He laughs. "Uh, yeah, Rook. We're not blind."

"Ronin's gonna be so mad."

"Hey, look at it this way, Rook. Ronin's been doing this for years now, longer than me, that's for sure. And if he tells you he's not turned on in those shoots, probably every single one of them, he's a liar. It's natural, it's sexy as hell, Rook. It's the whole purpose of erotic photography, right? If we're not turned on, we don't give Antoine what he's looking for. So as bad as Antoine feels about needing Spencer to make you feel that way, that's his job. To give you a partner who turns you on so he can get his photos."

I think about this for a few minutes as I scrub. Billy stands off to the side, not facing me so I have an illusion of privacy. "Do you sleep with them, Billy? After you're done? I mean, what's it mean afterward?"

He shrugs. "I sleep with some of them, sure. But sometimes it's just a thing, ya know? Just a physical reaction, and nothing more."

I finish up with the shower and Billy hands me a towel and walks me upstairs to the studio.

Just a job, Rook. It's just a job.

THIRTEEN

ROOK

Ford is back when I enter the studio, but he's on the other side of the room, sitting in a chair next to Director Larry looking at the wall of screens. I ignore him and walk over to Spencer. His shirt is back, but he's still got the board shorts on. "Are we modeling together for all the shoots, Spencer?"

He doesn't turn, just keeps messing with his brushes and paint. "Does it bother you?"

"Um." Does it? "No, it doesn't bother me, that's not the right word." My camera team zooms in on me. I guess this is what Larry is looking for, because I can hear a tinny voice coming out of the earpiece of my main camera guy. "I'm just worried about what Ronin will think."

Spence turns now. "Ronin will just have to learn to deal, Rook. I picked you because you're beautiful, you're the girl I want to represent my bikes. And if that makes Ronin uncomfortable, too bad. I won't be in all the shots, but we have to get a few, at least. I mean, that's just reality, Rook."

MANIC

"I know," I say, sighing. "I should just forget about Ronin, huh?"

Spencer laughs. "Why? Why would you say that?" He points me over to the sheet and grabs his stuff, then starts painting my breast. "You like him, he likes you. What's the fucking problem?"

"If our roles were switched and Ronin was the model being painted up by a sexy artist, I'd be mad. I'd never put up with it, to be honest."

"So, you think I'm sexy, eh?"

I laugh. "You know what I mean."

"Well, you can't change that, Rook. You're the model, I'm the artist, he's the boyfriend. He can deal or not. But I'm still the artist and you're still the model. And if he's smart he'll just shut the fuck up about it, stay out of the way until the contract is over, and then forget it ever happened."

"Do you have a girlfriend?"

He winces.

"What?"

"She broke up with me."

"How come?" I suck in a small breath as he paints a string along my upper ribcage and around my back.

He ignores my question for so long I'm ready to ask it again when he finally looks up, smiling.

"What?"

"She broke up with over this contract. She was jealous."

I can't help but laugh with him. "Well, I guess she didn't mean much, huh? You don't look broken up about it."

"Well, I do miss her hands because she's the one responsible for my body art. But I'm not a relationship kinda guy, Rook. I like to play the field. So if she wants to be a bitch about it, get jealous over you and me spending so much naked time together, then she can take the fuck off."

"Have you known her long?"

"Yeah, she's the model in all the other pictures too."

"Holy crap! That's just rude, Spencer!"

He doesn't even look up from painting my nipple. "What's rude?"

"She's your model and you chose me!"

He shrugs. "Your name's Rook and in case you haven't noticed, I've got quite a thing for blackbirds going on. Besides, this was a business decision. She wanted the contract money, that's all. She allowed me to paint her so she could make money. I let her be my canvas because she was willing. She used me, I used her, and to tell you the truth"—he does look up now—"I'm pretty fucking pissed off that she turned it all personal. I never promised her this contract and as you now know, this is way beyond a modeling job, right? It's a TV show, it's a marketing campaign, it's my entire fucking business. And if everything goes well, you'll be part of this franchise for a long time. I have long-term plans, Rook. And she was never part of them."

"But I am?"

"That's right," he says in a soft whisper. "You're definitely part of them."

Both our sound guys move the mics closer to us and I can only hope they missed that last part. Because I think Spencer Shrike just made some kind of declaration to me and I'm having hard time thinking it was professional because now his paintbrush is practically caressing me between my legs. He uses broad strokes, so it's not like he's trying to excite me on purpose, but he's a man, kneeling down in front of me, staring at my most private body parts.

I inhale, close my eyes, and think about how I'd feel if I walked in on Ronin doing this to some girl. Or even worse, Ronin getting his manly parts painted up by some hottie chick.

I snicker internally, proud of myself. That image was all it took.

"OK, on the floor with you, Blackbird."

I cringe. I was mad the last time he painted up my girly parts, but now I'm confused. And worried about Ronin and my physical reaction to Spencer.

MANIC

"Problem, Rook?"

"No," I say as I kneel down, then lie back and fold my hands over my stomach. The camera crew backs off for this and it makes me wonder if Ford told them to do that. The first bikini was just white, so Spencer didn't spend a lot of time down here. It was quick and easy. The second one only required that he paint the stripes on.

But this time I'm bare again and Spencer wants to paint the suit up to look iridescent, so he spends more time than he did the last two times put together.

"Hurry up, Spencer, this is weird. If Ronin was here, he'd be having a fit, you staring right up into my—"

"Hey now! I'm painting, Rook!"

I snort. "Whatever, I'm standing up in ten seconds. I'm not spreading my legs for your motorcycle ad, so you don't need to get carried away with the details down there."

When my private count gets to ten, I push his head back and stand up. "I wasn't kidding."

He ignores me and continues painting a shadow under the string that wraps around my hip to the little piece of fabric on my ass.

"I don't like doing more than one outfit in a day. This sucks. I'm ready to be done—"

"We still have one more, Rook. Better settle down, sister."

My irritation comes out as a growl. "Well, I don't like it. I'm hungry, I want to pee, I'd like to take a nap, or read a fucking book, or—"

"Here, Rook."

Ford is standing a little behind me thrusting a tablet in my direction. I take it automatically. "What's this?"

"Books. I like thrillers and classics, so maybe not your thing, but you can shop the store and find something you like."

"Oh." I take a moment to calm down from my rant and then smile. "Thanks, Ford. I definitely need to get one of these. In fact, I need to go shopping, maybe I need a car? When will Elise be back? I'm tired of hanging out with men, why can't this show have more girls on it? And what's up with having no girls on the production team too? Not one girl can run a microphone or camera?"

I get silence. Straight-up crickets.

"Hello? Are you guys listening to me?"

"No!" they all say at once. Even Director Larry's team on the other side of the room yells it out.

"Well, shit. I guess I better find me a book then." I open the leather flap that covers the device and it comes to life. I swipe my fingers to unlock it, then browse the little carousel that holds all Ford's books.

Talk about eye-opening. "Ford's reading *Gatsby, Deeply Odd*, and *Making Babies for the Billionaire*." I get snorts from everyone, even my team.

"Funny, Rook," Ford says dryly from across the room.

"You know what's funnier? The fact that all you dumbasses got the joke. I know what you're reading at night."

"Someone please, turn on the fucking tunes."

"Spencer, that was not nice. How about I read from the billionaire book? You guys should like that."

Spencer stops painting and looks up at me. "Does he really have that on there?"

We all bust out laughing. "Oh, Spencer."

"All right, I'm done. Let's get this over with, give you something else to bitch about for a while."

I race out and head straight to the bathroom, then make my way upstairs, totally oblivious to the fact that I'm one hundred percent naked. It was less than a month ago that I stood in the Chaput dressing room wondering how all the girls could just walk around naked, but here I am, traipsing around the entire building like that.

My team is waiting for me upstairs and Spencer is shirtless again, but he's changed into some faded jeans with holes and grease all over them, like he's been working in a garage all day.

MANIC

He's sitting casually on the new bike, messing with the grips as he chats to Billy. This bike is like psychedelic. It's got swirls of light blue and purple on the frame and the tank. The Shrike logo is a thick bold black outline, the total opposite of the girly one from the last shoot. The set is still beachy, but the backdrop spills over onto the floor and it makes it look like we're on the side of a road. When I sit down for Josie, she takes off my blonde wig and exchanges it for a black one. The cut is shorter now, the bangs severe, and it frames my face. She removes the old makeup and paints on new. This time I get the glossy treatment. Red lips, dark eyes, and plum blush.

I also get some spiky pumps that probably require a personal injury insurance policy to walk in, and after about thirty minutes I'm stumbling my way over to the guys.

Antoine is in his office, and when I'm ready Billy goes to get him.

"What's all this?" I fan my arms out to the set, curious as to what message we're sending.

"You're a hitchhiker, I'm your knight in shining armor."

"I'm hitchhiking in a bikini and fuck-me pumps?"

"Biker fantasy, Rook. Trust me."

"O-kaaaay."

Antoine and Billy appear, and as usual, Billy does all the talking. I wonder how I'm going to fill in a whole evening of conversation when Antoine and I go to dinner. I wonder if he'll take me to Cookie's. I'm so fucking hungry.

"You're thumbing, Rook, step behind the bike and act the part."

I do as I'm told, then pretend to have a conversation with Spencer as he ogles my tits. I'm not sure if that's pretend or not, but it makes me frown and Antoine barks out something harsh and Billy tells me to look happy. I do, then climb in front of Spencer, facing him, and wince as I realize I'm in yet another position that will have Ronin breaking up with me as soon as he gets back. Spencer sneaks a peek down.

"Really, Spence? I mean, you've been looking at my goods all day, you haven't seen enough?"

"That's totally different, I'm not supposed to get turned on when I'm painting, but this is different."

"*Spencer.*"

Spencer glares at Antoine this time. "Look, she asked me a question, *again*. So why does she get to talk to me, but I'm not allowed to talk to her?"

"Who said you're not allowed to talk to me?"

"Antoine. I'm supposed to keep it professional, but that's a fucking first. The whole reason we hired you, Antoine, was because you're famous for getting the girls to be as unprofessional as possible."

"OK, let's just move on. What should I do? You're the one in charge, Spencer. I need direction here because I'm not all that good at this shit."

Spencer shoots Antoine a look. "See, she wants me to tell her what to do." He looks at me, his hands wrap around my middle, then slip down to the top of my ass. "Take the pictures, Antoine," Spencer growls.

I hold down a laugh because these babies have no idea what to do with me right now.

Antoine starts shooting and Spencer's one hand stays down, while the other one slides up, picks up my arm and drapes it over his shoulder, then cups my breast. "Kiss me again, Rook."

I look at him, the shock plastered across my face, I'm sure. I swallow, not sure what to do with myself right now, either.

"Rook," Spencer repeats, a little harsher now. "I want kissing, I want mad fucking passionate kissing. The kind of kissing I've seen in all those other photos of you, the kissing that is so filled with emotion and longing and lust, I'm instantly hard. Kiss me like that, Blackbird."

I gulp some air and stare at him, right into his eyes. We hold that moment as Billy translates encouraging things from Antoine. I lean in a little, slowly, never breaking eye contact, then

MANIC

touch his lips with a soft kiss, and pull back.

He smiles.

I do it again and this time he's ready, his hand leaves my breast and wraps around my head, pulling me towards him. His mouth opens and I respond by doing the same. Our tongues flick against each other, then I pull back as his grip releases, trying to catch my breath.

"That's more like it," he whispers. "Now turn around, Rook."

I stand up and turn around, my ass against his thighs.

He's very excited.

His hands go to my shoulders, then his fingertips drag down my arms. One hand grabs my breast, while the other slides across my stomach, then drops very low.

"Arch your back and tip your head, Rook."

I do, and his hand drops even lower with the change in my body position. I have to admit, for being a bike designer, he's pretty good at this sexy modeling stuff. His mouth is suddenly heavy against my neck, his breath slow, but louder than before.

I moan.

Oops.

He laughs behind me and I relax a little.

We're still acting, I tell myself.

FOURTEEN

ROOK

Billy follows me downstairs to the shower room again and this makes me wonder. "What's the deal with this whole bodyguard thing, Billy? How come you have to follow me around?"

"Rook, this building is unlocked during business hours, you do realize that, right?"

"Um…"

"I wasn't gonna say anything because you've got enough going on here today, but Antoine was pissed that you didn't wait for me to walk you to the bathroom. You can't just traipse around naked outside the studio. At the very least, have your camera crew around. You need to wait for someone to go with you, even if it's just walking upstairs."

"Oh, well, yeah, that makes sense." I can't argue with that. It was a little weird walking around naked all alone, anyway. "Thanks, Billy. I'm really glad you're here. It makes a difference."

He smiles and turns around. "Hurry up, I'm starving and we can't eat until we're done. Hopefully the next painting will go fast."

"Oh," I say, squeezing out the sponge and rubbing down my chest. "Are you coming with us to dinner? Ronin just said I was eating with Antoine tonight."

Billy laughs. "Antoine doesn't go anywhere with the models alone. Ever. Not even you, Rook. He keeps a healthy distance from all of them, that's why he's got Ronin. To run interference."

"Makes sense, I guess." I scrub the bikini bottoms off my front and then get as much of my ass as I can before holding the sponge out to Billy. "Get the rest of it, hurry."

He does as I ask and I just have to privately shake my head at what my life has become. It's weird. All these guys looking at me naked. Getting my picture taken. Being a sort of girlfriend to Ronin, yet my job is allowing his former best friend to touch and kiss me. And Billy here, washing paint off my backside.

"OK," he says, turning me around so the water washes off the soap. "You're good. Let's go." He hands me my towel, I wrap myself up again, and we go back to the art room.

Ford is back in his director's chair in the corner of Spencer's space, Spencer is messing with the music, and Team Rook is looking tired and bored. I'd hate to be the camera person for a reality show. It's like you do nothing but hang out until something exciting happens. Even Ford looks bored out of his mind. He's holding the tablet in his lap, reading.

I walk over to him. "*Gatsby, Odd,* or *Billionaire?*"

He grins and I notice that there's a dimple in his chin when the smile reaches his eyes. "Guess."

"*Gatsby,*" I say.

"Correct."

I shrug, "It was the first one on the carousel."

"Do you like *Gatsby,* Rook?"

"Never read it. I pretty much dropped out of school at sixteen, so I never got past *Lord of the Flies.*" He's scowling at me. "What?"

"You didn't finish high school?"

"I took the GED. Why? Is there an educational requirement to pose naked with bikes?"

"It surprises me, that's all. You come off as smart, like I said earlier."

Yeah, Ronin likes the dumb ones. I shake my head at him. "You know, Ford, every time I start to like you, you act like a pretentious asshole."

He points his finger at me. "See, that right there is what trips me up. Most drop-outs don't use the word pretentious."

"Never mind him, Blackbird, disrobe, let's go. This is a one-piece, let's get a move on."

Ford huffs out a laugh under his breath.

"What?" I ask, looking back at him again.

"You'll see," is all he says.

Ford chats with me as Spencer paints, calling out book titles to see if I'd like to read them. He starts with classics, none of which appeal to me. He turns his nose up at every rejection, like he's taking it personally. Which I can totally see. He looks like a classics lover.

"Just skip to the romance, Ford. Why torture yourself?"

"Billionaires?"

I laugh at that, along with Spencer's new fascination with my armpits. He's painting bikini strings in very interesting places. "No, I'm not into fantasy billionaires. I've got Ronin, remember?"

My team chuckles at this dig. I think I like my team, they seem to be on my side.

"Right, yes, I do recall that."

"Just try the regular romances, or the ones they write for kids my age."

He cringes at the word kid, but fuck it. Why pretend? I'm still a kid. I like being a kid, I missed a lot of kid time in my earlier life, and I'm in no hurry to grow up now, even if I am standing here naked in front of a whole room full of men.

Ford's brow twists a little as he searches. "Coming-of-age or college life?"

MANIC

"Um, the last one I guess. Just read the description for the number one book, let's start there."

"*Ashley, the only virgin in her freshman dorm…*" He stops and looks up at me. "Seriously?"

"Keep going, it sounds good." My team is having a hard time hiding their amusement now.

"*… is desperate to be deflowered by long-time crush, Eaton Fuller.* Eaton? What kind of name is that?"

"Says the guy named Ford."

"*But that's before hot and dangerous Rowdy Breaker saves her from a spelunking adventure gone wrong.* This is stupid. Spelunking gone wrong? It's so cliché."

"One-click that sucker, Ford. Any guy called Rowdy has gotta be hot. You don't get to be number one for no reason. I'll read about Rowdy and his cave-dwelling tendencies. Hand it over."

"We're done here, no time for books, Rook."

"Done? You just started!"

Ford laughs.

I look down and if this suit was real, it'd be nothing but a bunch of rope winding around my body in strategic places. None of which happens to cross my private parts. "This isn't a bathing suit, it's rope. I look like I'm being tied up for… Oh."

They are all laughing at me now.

"Come on," Spencer says. "I'll walk you up."

"Are you modeling with me this time, too?"

Snickers from Team Everybody.

"What?"

"Nope, not me this time, Rook. Billy's got this privilege."

Billy is the sexiest cowboy I've ever seen. I've never pretended the guy wasn't gorgeous to look at, because he is very easy on the eyes. But sporting all that western gear, the tight jeans, the hat, the chaps, and the boots, in combination with a new rough expression I've never seen him wear before, plus his bare chest, makes him look like he's about to bind my wrists and take me from behind.

Whew. I have to stop and take a breath after that thought.

This bike is a work of art. It's got a custom seat shaped like a western saddle and an entire scene depicting a bad-boy cowboy meets helpless half-naked female airbrushed on the top of the fat tank. The whole frame is a smoky black with barbed-wire running down the fenders like racing stripes.

"Wow."

"I love this bike, Rook," Spencer says as he stands next to me. "I've been waiting to get decent images of this one and put it online. It's not a showroom model, but a one-of-a-kind custom. I'll be sorry to sell it actually." He laughs a little under his breath. "Until I get the check, that is. Because this one's a sweet ninety-five grand."

Holy shit.

"Over here, Rook," Josie calls.

I walk over to the salon and she removes the makeup from the last shoot and reapplies. I get another wig, only this time it's Farrah Fawcett à la Charlie's Angels hair, all frosted blonde highlights in big bouncy curls that fall halfway down my back. I get the natural look as far as makeup goes, and then I slip my feet into the cowgirl boots and plop the hat on my head.

When I walk back over to the guys Spencer buckles a gun holster around my waist and then slides two revolvers inside.

So I'm wearing boots, guns, and a hat. And my body has been painted to look like I've been tied up.

When I look up to see what's next, every mouth is hanging open.

Except Antoine's, because he's just coming out of his office, trying to pretend I'm fully clothed.

"What're you assholes looking at? I've been walking around here naked all day, quit it!"

MANIC

They mumble out some incomprehensible words as I walk over to Billy.

He's smiling. "That is fucking hot for some reason. I'm not sure why, it just is, Rook."

I shrug. "You're pretty hot too, Billy. Maybe it's the hats?"

He chuckles. "Yeah, the hats. OK, for this one you're my bitch. So bend the fuck over the seat, ass to the camera, and let me whack you a few good ones so your cheeks turn pink."

"*What?*"

"I'm kidding, Rook." He sits down on the western saddle seat and pulls me toward him. "Just sit in my lap to start, wrists together, because if you do that, you'll see it looks like I've bound you up."

I put my wrists together, then Billy reaches down and adjusts them. He puts his arm around me as Antoine starts the shoot. Billy is not Spencer, he knows exactly what to do and when to do it, so I relax and just do as I'm told. I lean against him as his hands rub the side of my body in long strokes. He leans down and begins nibbling on my neck and then whispers in my ear. "Antoine liked that moaning you did last time, but he's not gonna ask for it, Rook. So give the man his photos and you'll be done sooner. That's the secret to this job. Give him what he wants and right now he wants you to look the same way with me as you do with Ronin."

"Can I move my hands? Or do I have to pretend to be tied up?"

"Do you want to move them?"

"Yes."

He repositions my body so I'm straddling the tank, leaning back on his chest like I was with Spencer. Billy has either had a lot of bike sex before, or he's got a very creative on-the-fly imagination because I'm pretty hot and bothered in a matter of seconds. He opens my legs right up, places one on the handlebars, and then reaches around to cup my breast. "Touch me, Rook."

I reach back and grab his head, thrusting my upper body

up and out. Billy's right hand caresses the leg propped up on the handlebar, then slides down and slips right up under my ass. His other hand is squeezing my breast until I squirm from the pressure. "Turn towards me, Rook." His voice is a low rumble.

I turn and his mouth is right there, his kisses just as passionate as any Ronin gave me, and his hands just as daring. His fingers are between my legs, not past any point of no return, but hovering right there, right on the edge. He rubs my lower abdomen a little, slips down, then brings his fingertips back up just when I think he's gonna slip them in farther.

It's driving me fucking crazy. I am so horny right now it's not even funny.

I lose track of time, of the camera, of everyone in the room. I feel his kisses, I kiss him back, but I'm not even inside my body right now, that's how worked up he has me. I'm not sure what it means, but none of this can be good for a brand-new relationship with a man who is not the one fondling me right now.

"OK, great shots, Billy and Rook. We're done for today."

And that's it. Antoine takes his camera and walks away.

"You OK, Rook?" Billy asks, his voice totally normal, like he always is after a shoot.

"Um…" *Wow.*

He lifts me up off him and sets me on the ground. "Come on," he says, taking my hand as he gets off the bike. "I'll walk you to the showers."

I have no words as we go back downstairs. Like none.

We go in and he starts the shower for me. "You wanna talk about it?"

I blow some air out of my cheeks. "I don't think I can do this, Billy."

"What are ya talking about? You did great."

"I mean, I don't think I can keep all these feelings separate."

He laughs. "Oh, you're hot for me now?"

"No, it's just, that felt so…"

He grins as my words trail off. "It's OK to admit it, Rook."

MANIC

"Good, it felt good."

"It's supposed to feel good. That's what people want to see in the pictures."

"So you don't want to really jump my bones?"

"Well, fuck yeah I do, but you're seeing Ronin, right? So you're off limits. I'm not an asshole, I'd never do that."

I've got nothing for that response. I'm not sure if it helps or makes things worse.

"Rook, when I'm working, you're just a naked body, OK? And I guarantee you, Spencer is the same way. He's got a naked girl in his lap and he'd like to finish her off and get himself some too. That's just how it is. But when the shoot stops, you're Rook again. And that's not the same thing as a naked body in our laps. It's work, Rook. Not love."

He takes the sponge from me and starts washing my back and I just stand there and let him. When he's done he thrusts it at me until I take it from him. "You can finish now, right? I'll be in the hallway."

He walks out and leaves me standing there. I snap back to my senses and wash the rest of the paint off, then wrap myself up in a towel and go out to meet him. We walk upstairs together and then he drops me off in front of Ronin's door.

"Be ready in an hour, we're having dinner, remember?"

Right, dinner. I nod and go inside, ready to be alone so I can begin to process this day.

FIFTEEN

ROOK

Dinner with Billy and Antoine wasn't terrible, but I spent most of the time just listening to them talk about sports. It was pretty boring. And now that I'm back home in my apartment, I'm simply exhausted. I can't imagine working like this every day. My phone buzzes and I smile at Ronin's face on my screen.

"Geez," I say after answering, "I figured you forgot about me."

"Nah, I knew you were eating with Antoine, remember? How'd it go today?"

I hesitate. "Well, it was… weird, confusing, exciting, long, demanding, and… weird."

"Why weird twice?"

I thought about this conversation all through dinner. I need to get this out in the open, because if Ronin is gonna break it off with me over this contract, I might as well understand that now. "When you model with other girls, does it…"

"Does it what?"

"Feel good?"

MANIC

He lets out a small laugh but I'm not convinced that it's a happy one. "Did it feel good today with Billy and Spencer?"

"You knew I was modeling with them?"

"Rook, I'm your manager. I know what every painting looks like, we're not making this shit up as we go. This has all been planned. So yes, I know what you did today. And my question is, did it feel good?"

I swallow. "It did. I can't help it, when they're asking me to kiss them for the photo shoot it got personal. I felt turned on."

He says nothing for several long seconds.

"Do you get turned on when you're with other girls?"

"Yeah, I do."

"So, what I'm feeling is… normal?"

"It is."

"So you're OK with it?"

"Would you be OK with it? If it was me doing a contract like this?"

Oh God. He's totally breaking up with me.

"Rook? Would you?"

What do I say? *No, I'd break up with you.* Or, *Yes, I would, so you should be OK with this too.*

"Rook, it's not a hard question."

I take a deep breath and then let it out. "No, I wouldn't be OK with it."

"I'm not either, but it's too late for that. You signed, I decided to stand by you and wait it out, and this is what that looks like."

"Are you mad at me?"

"Yeah. I am, I'm not gonna lie, Rook. It pisses me off and it's even worse knowing I'm not there. Antoine isn't paying attention during the artwork, is he?"

"No, he's upstairs the whole time."

"So who's in there? Ford?"

"Yes."

"Spencer, obviously. Camera crews?"

"Yes, and the director people."

"Billy?"

"No, but he walks me to and from the studio and he's in charge of helping me wash the paint off." He grunts at this. "That was Antoine's call, Ronin. Not me. It was him or Spencer, and Antoine said Billy. And if it makes you feel any better, I'd prefer Billy because Billy knows exactly what he's doing and he keeps it professional."

"So Spencer tried something with you?"

"No! That's not what I said. It's just Billy understands this is pretend."

He lets out a long controlled breath but stays silent for a while. I have nothing to add, so I just let him think it through. "Well, I told you, Rook. I warned you and now it's all playing out exactly as I feared."

"What's that mean? I'm not interested in Spencer, Ronin. And I don't know what his deal is, but he's been one hundred percent professional with me during the painting. It's really only the photo shoots that bother me, because he wants me to kiss him and stuff."

Silence.

"Did you hear me?"

More silence.

"So we're fighting? That's what's happening?"

"What do you want me to say, Rook? It bothers me, but I'll get over it? Is that what you want to hear?"

"Well, yeah. That's perfect actually. But I know you're messing with me, so it's also pretty fucked up."

Silence again.

"So I'll see you Sunday, then?"

"Sunday, yeah. We'll be home late afternoon probably."

"I miss you. And you didn't even give me a chance to say anything when you said you loved me earlier."

"It just slipped out. Sorry."

Long, dreadful, agonizing silence.

Now what the hell am I supposed to do with that? "I'm tired,

MANIC

exhausted really, and Ford will be here at five to make me run stadiums with him, so I—"

"What?"

"Ford. I made a deal with him so I can use your apartment to shower and get some privacy. I hope that's OK."

"Which part," he growls, "the fact that you're running with Ford in the morning or using my apartment while I'm gone?"

"OK, I'm hanging up now." I press end on my phone and lie back on my bed. He's got every right to be mad but I don't have to listen to that shit.

My phone buzzes.

"What?"

"I'm sorry."

"Look, Ronin, let's just break up then, OK? Because as you pointed out to me the other night, I'm stuck. This job needs to get done. I'm committed to it, and there's nothing I can do. So let's just call it off and maybe we can try again later or maybe we just say fuck it. You can take care of Clare for the rest of your life and I can move on and go to school."

"Is that what you want?"

"Yes. Because I spent the whole fucking day worried about *you*, Ronin. I worried about every single thing I did, and even though Spencer told me I was being ridiculous and Billy assured me you would understand, I couldn't stop thinking about how mad you were gonna be. And I can't live like that. So, I won't use your apartment, OK? And you just take your time coming home. Bye."

I end the call and then look up and realize every single bit of this was just caught on camera. I stow my tears away until I make it outside and then I go sit under the cherry trees and cry.

It's one of those poor-me, silent and tearful, pity cries. And it gives me a headache. But this day has been too much for me all of a sudden and I can't hold it in. And the last thing I want is for Director Larry and his people to watch me fall apart after that stupid conversation.

I'm not sure how long I've been lying out here when the studio door opens. I listen to the click of expensive shoes across the concrete. "What now?" I say, annoyed.

Ford stops and looks down on me. "What are you doing?"

"Crying. What does it look like I'm doing? And I'm sure you guys got all that on camera, so don't waste my time with your feigned innocence, Ford. I'm not in the mood."

He smiles and sits down on a nearby picnic table. "See, feigned, that's another one. Most drop-outs don't use feigned, either."

"Go away."

"We were listening to the conversation, Rook."

I turn away from him and close my tired eyes. "Go away."

"Your phone's been buzzing since you hung up on him, so why not just go answer it?"

"I'm not running with you tomorrow, I don't need to take a shower up there anymore."

"You're just being bratty, Rook, he's jealous, that's all. Go inside or I'll have a technician come down and hang a camera." He gets up and walks away. "I'm dead serious about that, you have five minutes."

I wait until he goes back inside, then I count to sixty and get up to go back to my apartment. My phone has seven missed calls and no voicemail messages. I figure that means he's not interested in a call back, so I just turn the ringer off and slip into bed, fully clothed.

SIXTEEN

ROOK

Someone is rocking me back and forth. "Whaaaaaat?"
"It's almost five, Rook."
"Grrrr... Ford, I told you I'm not running with you because I'm not going to be using Ronin's shower."
"Right, but I have another offer you might be interested in."
I pull the covers over my head.
"I'll take the camera out of your bedroom."
I slide the cover back down. "Why? Why do you want me to run with you? It's weird. I know this is some sordid plot to make Ronin jealous and hate me even more. Go away."
He laughs. "Sordid, that's three. Where did you get that one?"
I open my eyes and stare up at him. Ford is a strange guy, but I have a good answer for him, so I say it. "*Sordid Lives*. Ever seen it? That movie is hi-*lar*-ious. I didn't actually know what sordid meant before that movie, but I looked it up."
"*Sordid Lives?*" he says with a little question mark at the end. "Unusual choice of movie for a girl your age."

MANIC

He sits down at the end of my bed and waits to see if I'll tell him anything else. I wasn't planning on it, but then I remember what his job actually is. He's a producer, he's into this stuff, he might, in fact, understand why I'm a movie freak. "I like comedies. They… always made me feel better." And this one is about white trash, and that's me in a nutshell. But I leave that part out.

His mouth makes an O, like that explains everything. "Come running, Rook. It's good for you."

"I'd rather pout."

He smiles and a chin dimple appears. "Yes, that's always fun for children, but you're a grownup, Rook. So get up and come running with me."

"That won't work, you know."

"What won't work?"

"That reverse psychology bullshit you're trying to pull on me. Call me a child, tell me I'm childish so I'll do what you ask. Run your ass off up and down those stairs to make me feel lazy so I'll put in more effort. It won't work, I'm not stupid."

"Well, I'll tell you what. Get up and mope along with me and tomorrow I'll show up with all kinds of statistics that will convince you this is good for you."

I pull the covers back over my head. "I'm too tired today. Yesterday was hard and long. I want to go back to sleep."

"Today will be quick, Rook. Antoine told Spencer just one outfit today, he's going up to see Clare and won't be back until Sunday. So you can take a nap after work."

"What? He's going up there and didn't even invite *me?*" That last word barely makes it out of my mouth before I'm crying. "Ronin never even said anything about Antoine going up today!"

"Rook, it's not a vacation, his niece is addicted to heroin, she's not doing well, he's sick with worry. It's got nothing to do with you."

I try to stop my crying because it's so embarrassing, but once I start holding it in I make weird noises. Ford drags the covers off me. "What the hell are you wearing?"

"Clothes."

"To bed?" He asks this with a weird cock-eyed look on this face.

I point up at the camera.

"OK." He pulls me by the feet and drags me until I fall off the bed. "Run with me every day and I'll take out all your apartment cameras."

"You will?"

"Yes," he says nodding. "You're not adjusting very well, Rook. Go change, I'll be outside."

He walks out and leaves me there on the floor. *Not adjusting well, my ass. I'm the queen of adjusting.*

I get up, find another sporty outfit, tug it on, then step outside and walk over to Ford. He's sitting at the picnic table over by the cherry trees, holding out a box to me as I approach.

"What's that?"

"Running shoes. You can't wear those things, Rook. They're unacceptable."

I look down at my Converse. Then peek in the box. And change shoes. Might as well look the complete part. We walk over to the stadium, minus the camera crew. I guess they figure they'll sleep in if they can't follow us inside. We start at the same place we did yesterday, Ford trucking up and down those stairs like a pro, me dragging my feet up while expending as little effort as possible.

I watch him to take my mind off Ronin. He runs hard, like he's really racing someone, or like he's running for his life. I make it almost nine rows before he stops, checks his watch, and then turns and heads back my way at the same break-neck pace. When he's only one row away I stop and wait.

He's breathing hard again, sweat dripping off his body. He takes off his shirt and starts wiping himself off.

"You need a towel, Ford."

He smiles. "Hungry?"

MANIC

I shrug. "Not so much this morning."

"Well, you might change your mind once you smell the food."

I follow him inside and this is a repeat from yesterday as well. Two breakfast burritos, two OJ's. We eat in complete silence and he doesn't make any move to start a conversation with me or even look uncomfortable because we're so quiet.

I think this is more of his reverse psychology, so I forbid my mouth from saying anything. He's not gonna win this, he won't.

When I'm done with my burrito, which did hit the spot even though I didn't think I was hungry, he simply picks up my trash, throws it away, then waits for me to get up and join him by the trashcan.

We walk back to the studio in silence and then he gives me a half-hearted goodbye at his car.

I go inside and go straight to Ronin's apartment to take a shower. I'm feeling like a creeper because I'm really not supposed to be in here today, but that's not enough to stop me from starting the water and taking off my clothes. I look at myself in the mirror and wonder if this mistake will ruin my life.

I press a bunch of random buttons on the shower control panel and wait to see if any good jets will come on. I don't like the rain shower, but I'm not really sure which button works that one, so sometimes it comes on and I have to press more random buttons until it stops. But this morning I get the steamy mist and two hard streams that come out of the corners and meet together to make one blaring jet of water. I stand underneath it and let it pound against my neck and upper back.

It feels good so I close my eyes.

A hand touches my shoulder and I whirl around. "AHHHHH!"

"Rook! It's me!" Ronin grabs me and pulls me towards him.

"You scared me!" The sudden rush of adrenaline has my heart pounding like a jackhammer and I really have to try hard not to cry. I put my hand over my face and take a few deep breaths.

"I'm sorry." He wraps his arms around me and holds me

against his chest. "I'm sorry, I didn't mean to scare you."

"What're you doing here?"

"It's my house, silly."

I pull away and enjoy his naked body for a second. God, Ronin has a terrific body. "But you never said you were coming home."

"I left in the middle of the night. I shouldn't have been an ass on the phone. Antoine is leaving this afternoon to see Clare, then coming home with Elise on Sunday. I told them I had to come home because I'm not at all interested in breaking up with you over this contract. I'm not happy about it, I'm not happy about Ford, or Spencer, or Billy or any of it, actually. But I'm not ready to say goodbye over something so *temporary*."

I hug him. "I'm so glad you're here. I don't want to break up with you, either. I just feel so guilty for what I have to do in those shoots."

"We'll get through it, OK?"

I nod into his chest.

He pries me from his body and grabs the soap. "We gotta get an early start, it's the sexy Elvis painting today. I'm gonna take over from here, if that's OK."

"Take over how?" I say as he lathers my arm with the soap.

"In the shoots. I called Spencer and told him I'd model with you, no pay."

"What—" His soapy hands move to my breasts and I lose track of my words.

"I don't need the money, believe me. It's not a big deal to work for free and I have to be around all day with you anyway, to keep an eye out. Besides," he says, rubbing my other breast now. "I'm not sure any man would call what I'm doing a job."

I look up at him and he leans down and kisses me gently. He drops the soap and pulls me right up against his full erection, still gently caressing my lips. My hands slip around his waist and then up his muscular back. I drag them back down his arms and then up his chest. He pulls me with him as he steps back a few paces, then sits down on the tiled bench on the far side of the shower, away from the punishing jets and right into the thick mist of steam coming from the ceiling.

He leans back against the wall and I climb into his lap, positioning my hips over his thickness, then easing down until he fills me up. We stay still like that for a few seconds, me leaning against him, my head on his shoulder, him dragging his hand down my wet hair, and then we start rocking. Just a little at first.

I close my eyes and tug on his hair a little, making him groan. He reaches up and fondles my breast, gently rolling my nipple between his fingertips. I pull my head back and look down, deep into his eyes. "Do you love me?"

He smiles. "I do."

"I wanted to tell you back, but you hung up."

"You scare me, Rook."

"Why?" I ask, puzzled.

"Because your future is making itself right now, this very moment. And you have no idea it's happening. I want you so completely it hurts. But you and I are in two totally different places."

My whole body shivers with a chill as I absorb his words. I swallow. "That sounds like the beginning of a break-up speech. Are you breaking up with me?"

He scoots my bottom closer, thrusting himself inside me a little more. "I love you, Rook. I'm not breaking up with you. But it's all bad timing, you know?"

I shake my head. "No, not really."

"My career started when I was seventeen. I've done everything you're just getting a taste of now. I've traveled all over the world, I've made a shitload of money, I have pretty much everything I want."

"But—"

"Except the only thing I really want."

I wait for it, but he lets out a long sigh and holds it in. "Is it a secret?"

He lets out a soft laugh and rocks himself into me again. "No, it's not. I already told you that night we went to the zoo."

"A family," I say, a little breathless now because what he's doing, this serious conversation combined with the sensual lovemaking, is making my heart pound.

"Yes. I'm done, Rook. I can live off the money I've made for decades. I'm ready to do something else. Start something new."

"Well, how is that a problem for us?" I ask, lifting up and slipping down on him. It's his turn to become breathless. "I'm not against the idea, you know."

He smiles as his hand reaches up to cup my breast.

I shiver again, but this time it's a good one.

"Not against the idea is not the same as on board." His fingers stop and his hands wrap around my waist as he slides me back and forth across his lap. My whole body flushes with heat and I tip my head back and close my eyes.

"I'm looking for a partner."

I swallow. "I'd like to be that partner, but—"

He waits.

I open my eyes. He's watching me very closely, his hands still gliding over my body, slowly—so, so slowly. My clit throbs against his friction.

He waits.

"I'm scared too, Ronin. But of very different things."

He wraps his arms around me completely and buries his face in my neck, tasting the water on my skin left over from the misting shower spray. "I'll take care of you, Rook."

I take a deep breath and let it out. "I want you to take care of me, Ronin."

His palms slide up underneath my wet hair and then he fists it, just a little, like a claim. It makes me hesitate, but then he pulls me forward until my cheek touches his. "Then let me, just let me put it all together for us. I can make you happy."

Our rocking becomes thrusting, just small movements at first, and then more forceful. I lift up and then ease down on

MANIC

him, making him growl a little. I smile at that, do it again, then again. His left hand fists my hair just as the other slips down to my neck, not a squeeze, but a gentle full palming against my throat, soft and light.

I don't panic at this move. He's done it before and it's always this gentle.

I know him now.

His hand continues down to my breast where he squeezes my nipple until I turn into his mouth and his tongue flicks against mine. My whole body is aching with these small touches. My hips continue their movement, but now I lean forward and then pull back, resting my forearms on his muscular shoulders as I rub myself against him.

He knows me now, too. He knows what I want, what I like. His fingers leave my breast and trace down my stomach, stopping at my crease. He slides his thumb back and forth against that tender spot and I bite my lip as the pleasure rockets up my body.

His other hand drags down my back and slips under my ass, urging me to lift up higher and rock down with even more force.

I let him guide me because even though I'm on top, he's in control.

He's always in control.

He pushes his thumb against my clit, hard, then soft again, repeating the pattern, knowing it drives me wild. I can feel the wave building in me and he does too, so he pulls back and makes me whimper.

"No, Ronin. Stay where you are."

He laughs softly into my ear, his breath hot. My whole back arches, opening myself up to him and then his thumb is back, pushing and making the little nub pulsate against him. He leans down as my arching back thrusts my breasts up to him, and he responds to the invitation by sucking on a nipple.

I lose it. The pulsations turn into short bursts, then explosions. He rocks me up and down harder, more forcefully, then growls against my neck, biting me just hard enough to make me squeal when he releases into me.

We stay still for a second, breathing hard, our hearts hammering against each other.

"Mmmmm," I say.

"Mmm-hmmm," he responds. "I'll make you a deal, Gidget."

I push my face into his neck, my tongue playing with his earlobe. "What deal?" I say, my blow of breath just enough get a tiny shiver out of him.

"You don't pose with anyone else but me and I won't pose with anyone else but you."

"Oh, I like that deal. That deal sounds like a deal."

"And after this contract, we walk away from modeling."

I sit up straight and look down at him. "Serious? But what about Antoine? Your job here?"

"I actually do have a degree, Rook. I didn't go to college to be King of the Closet, it was just too good of an opportunity to pass up. But we can talk about it after this contract is over, OK? Forget about everything and let me handle it. Can you do that?"

I let out a huge sigh of relief. After yesterday I'm not sure being in control of everything is the way to go. Sure, I still like making my own decisions, but I'm an amateur in this business. Everyone seems to be in on the joke besides me. It would be so much better to let Ronin deal with things.

"I can do that."

He kisses me on the nose and slaps my ass, the smack echoing off the shower walls. That probably shouldn't make me giggle, but it does.

He grins at me with a knowing smile. "All right then, let's go get this job over with, then we can do this again when I wash all that paint off you."

SEVENTEEN

ROOK

Everything about this day is different. The mere presence of Ronin changes attitudes and actions. Ford never appears in the art studio and the camera and sound guys are never even supposed to get within ten feet of me. "They have zoom lenses for a reason, Rook," is what Ronin says. Plus, and this really makes me feel stupid, they're not even allowed to shoot me full frontal during painting, only when I'm on exhibition.

That phrase sucks, by the way.

Ronin knows all this stuff and I don't. Of course, I should probably be mad he didn't warn me, he *is* my manager. But whatever. It was my fault for not reading the contract properly. Pretty much everything about this contract is my fault for that reason alone.

Ronin sits off to the side as Spencer paints me up. Spencer is the same, he was never out of bounds during painting. And this outfit is quite interesting.

"Have you done this one before, Spence? You're quick this

time."

He looks up from painting the sparkly sequins on the bodice and winks. "I painted Veronica up like slutty Elvis about a dozen times."

"Veronica, that's the girlfriend who didn't get the job?"

"Yeah, we did the Elvis Fest in Vegas last year. She won a pretty big costume contest, even though she's a girl and she wasn't even wearing a costume. That was hysterical, people were pissed. But hey, you can't deny the talent of these fingers."

I look over at Ronin and he's smiling and shaking his head.

"Do you miss her?"

He stops painting. "Little bit. But not enough to give her a job as the Shrike Girl just because she's my girlfriend. And it pissed me off that she wanted that contract so bad she'd fight with me over it. I liked her for her, she liked me for Shrike Bikes."

I have nothing to say to that. I doubt it's true because Spencer is very good-looking and he seems like a funny and easy-going guy, but what do I know? Maybe she's a total gold-digger and he's right?

"Anyway," Spencer continues, "I've painted this outfit more than any of the others. And the bike that goes with it is pretty fucking cool as well."

"Does the bike have a cape?"

He laughs. "No."

"Do I get a cape?"

"Yes."

"Oh, I like that. I'm like a super-sexy naked Elvis girl."

"Yeah, and thanks to your temper tantrum last night, I get Ronin the supermodel as your Elvis counterpart for free." Spencer looks over at Ronin, clicks his tongue, and shoots him with his finger.

"Right," Ronin replies. "But from now on the only lap super-sexy naked Rook will be sitting in is mine." He shoots Spencer back. "So I win."

Spencer mumbles under his breath.

"Are you guys friends again?"

Mumbles from both of them.

"OK, let's change the subject. Let's talk about Ford. Why don't Ronin and Ford get along?" I hear people muttering behind me, back where Director Larry is with Ford. "What'd Ford do?"

No one wants to tackle that one because all I get is silence.

"OK, moving away from things that require you men to talk about your feelings. How'd you get started doing this painting stuff, Spence?"

"Took art since I was a kid. But you know how you were born looking like a model?"

"Yeah." That's true too. I didn't do anything to look this way. It's just how it is.

"Well, I was born to paint up naked girls. That's the only explanation I have for it. I know how to do it, I know how to mix up colors, and I see perspective. I've taken lots of classes and even did a fancy summer apprenticeship with a big-name *trompe l'oeil* body paint artist. She was pretty cool and she never took students, but my dad paid her well, and I wasn't too stupid—her words, not mine. Plus, she was French, and I already spoke French by that time, thanks to Ronin. But, mostly, I just always knew how to do this shit, Rook. Everyone has one God-given gift and painting naked girls is mine. Maybe I'm not curing cancer, but whatever. This is what I got, so I just needed someone to point me in the right direction and show me how to use the gift."

"So you majored in art at school?"

He almost snorts. "*No*, are you kidding? My old man is a filthy rich bastard, but private university prices for finger-painting was beyond even his wasteful tendencies."

"So what'd you major in?"

He looks up at me. "Business, what else? You can't run a business without knowing what the fuck you should do with it."

"Well, you're pretty good at this business stuff, Spence. You have a lot going on professionally. What'd you major in, Ronin?"

Ronin just smiles, like he's keeping a secret.

MANIC

"What was it, Spencer? Accounting, right?" I look over at Ronin and wink. "Spencer the Businessman Biker and Top Model Ronin the Accountant. Seems about right."

"Marketing," Ronin says. "I majored in marketing. And that's what I'm gonna do when we quit after this contract."

"Quit?" Spencer is appalled. "You're not quitting, are you, Rook?"

"Afraid so. We're done. Gonna buy a minivan and get desk jobs."

Spencer looks over to Ronin. "Did you do this on purpose?"

"Do what?" I ask.

Spencer stands up and puts a hand towards my face. "Hold on, Rook." He walks over to Ronin. "Did you talk her out of the next deal I was gonna offer? That was confidential."

"I didn't talk her out of anything, Spencer. And as far as I know, she has no idea what the next deal is."

"What deal?"

Spencer ignores me. "I told you, motherfucker. I wanted her for *all* the deals."

Oh shit, what just happened?

"And I told you, she's my fucking girlfriend. She's not a goddamn toy to parade around your shop for the next few years."

"Wait, what?"

Spencer takes a deep breath and then comes back to me. "OK, Rook, since Asshole over there pretty much ruined the surprise, I might as well tell you. If they like how things go in Sturgis and we give them a compelling reason to believe this show will fly, they're gonna offer us a twelve-episode season contract and we'll start filming in September. What we're doing right now is the two-hour pilot. It's a test, really. So if we got that deal, I was gonna ask you to come work for me up in the shop."

"Doing what? Sitting in the showroom naked?"

"Not the showroom, the *shop*. Where I build the bikes."

"But I don't build bikes, Spencer, so what would my job be?"

"Parts girl. You're like a pick-up girl, drive around and get us stuff, drop frames and tanks off at the painters, answer the phone and talk to clients."

"Hmmm." I think about it. I picture myself doing all that normal boring stuff, then look over at Ronin. "It's not modeling. Are you against this?"

I can tell by the look on his face he is, but he's in professional mode right now. "We'll talk about it in private, Rook."

Spencer growls at that answer but just goes back to work on the belt. The rest of the session is very quiet and very tense, but he was almost done anyway, so we're ready for Antoine before it gets old.

This time Ronin is the one who walks me upstairs.

If Elvis was a bike, he'd be this bike. It's even got lights on it—all sorts of gold and white and blue lights, and of course it's painted white, just like the outfit I'm wearing. I catch a glimpse of myself in a mirror and I look so much better than I did yesterday in those bikinis. This outfit is like Elvis if he were a girl and he had on a sexy one-piece bathing suit covered in gems instead of a bell-bottomed jumpsuit. I have the huge sparkly belt, the long pointed collar wrapping around my neck, and just as I'm starting to wonder where the cape is, Ronin appears and shakes it at me.

"Sexy, huh?"

I nod. It really is.

"OK, Rook. Sit for Josie and I'll go change and get ready."

Oh, my heart flutters at that. Ronin in a costume. Josie is watching me as I approach and take my seat in her chair.

"Yeah," she says. "No offense, I'm not sure if you're the jealous type, but seeing Ronin dressed up for his jobs is like the best perk this place has."

I laugh. "Well, I probably should be jealous, but I'm too busy picturing him all up as Elvis!"

We giggle at that and suddenly I wonder if Josie and I could be friends. She starts brushing my hair and I decide to fill in the silence.

"Are you married, Josie?"

MANIC

"Thirteen years now," she says brightly. "So when you finally meet my husband, hush on the fawning over Ronin stuff. All the boyfriends and husbands around here think us girls are secretly in love with Ronin." She winks. "But it's no secret, Rook. We are!"

I laugh at that too. I can see why. Ronin is a total catch. "Do you have kids, Josie?"

"Four."

"Really? But you look so young and I'd never be able to tell, you're so tiny and cute."

"You have the model genes and I have the baby-making genes." She shrugs. "I like it, so I'm not bitter about starting out as a teen mom. My husband was my high-school sweetheart. We weren't all that bright and well, let's just say I wasn't partying on my graduation night, I was seven months pregnant.

"We got married, and you'd think we were doomed, but it all worked out. I went to beauty school and landed a job here with Antoine and Elise almost right away. And we own a tow-truck business. That's how I met Elise, actually. She was the night dispatcher for us around the same time she was trying to decide if Antoine was the right guy for her. She said she'd give him a chance if he gave me a chance. I was just getting ready to graduate beauty school, no experience or references. And, well, the rest is history."

She's standing in front of me doing makeup and I can just tell she's thinking about her life. All the years that she's spent here in this studio. How Elise changed her luck, maybe.

"Elise is a good person, isn't she?"

Josie smiles. "She's the best, Rook. The absolute best."

I knew this the day I met her. Before she offered me the fake shampoo girl job and saved me from homelessness. I knew Elise was nice by the way she talked to me when she took me into her salon and washed my hair.

But it would've been so great to get a second opinion from someone I trusted. It would've been nice to go grab coffee with a best friend or a mom so I could run everything by them first.

Since I don't have a mom—and even if she was still alive she'd be the last person to ask for advice—and since I have no friends to double check my decisions with either, I decide to trust Josie's opinions instead. Almost everyone who works for Antoine and Elise has worked here for a significant amount of time. I think that counts as a reference.

EIGHTEEN

ROOK

R onin is hot.
Ronin is so fucking hot dressed up as Elvis, I can't keep my hands off him as we sit here on the amazing Shrike Elvis bike. The lights are blinking, Antoine's camera is going crazy, the shutter snapping like wild as he captures this mood we're in, and I'm about to abso-fucking-lutely lose control.

My fingertips trace down Ronin's chest, then begin unbuttoning his shirt.

"I never knew you had a thing for Elvis, Gidge," Ronin says playfully.

I lick my lips as his hands slip inside my cape and grab my ass. I have no idea what we're supposed to be doing on this bike, but no one seems to care that we're just sitting here flirting. The camera keeps clicking and the one time I managed to pry my eyes away from Ronin I-am-sexier-than-Kurt-fucking-Russell-in-*3000-Miles-to-Graceland* and glance at Spencer, his teeth are practically glinting in the sunshine, that's how big his smile is.

MANIC

He catches my gaze. "Now this, Rook, is what I'm talking about. I'm gonna sell a shitload of bikes with this shoot!"

I continue my task of undressing Ronin, ignoring Ronin's question about Elvis and Spencer's remark about sex selling bikes, but Ronin's still talking. "I mean, shit, Gidge, I might have to wear a costume everyday if this is what it does to you."

I laugh a little, but nothing will deter me from getting him out of this shirt right now. The last button comes undone and I slip the shirt down his shoulders a little. I suddenly notice Antoine's positive remarks. Of course, I don't understand them, but his tone is pretty clear. He's happy with my performance today as well.

I go for that big belt next, unclasping it and letting it drop to the floor with a thud, then drag the shirt down his arm, the pads of my fingertips caressing his biceps as they fall with the shirt sleeve.

He withdraws his arm and then I repeat this move on the other side, so the shirt drops to the floor next to the belt.

Now we're both naked on top, but being dressed up in paint makes it hard for me to consider myself nude. I *feel* dressed.

Overdressed, in fact.

As is Ronin.

When I look up Ronin's eyebrows are lifted up to his forehead. "What?"

He stretches out, easing himself down on the back fender, blue and yellow light flickering against his face. "Go for it, Gidge."

I lean down on his chest, moving forward just a little, just enough to tease myself, then sit back up, the palms of my hands dragging along his chest, across his abdomen, and then to the snap on his Elvis pants.

It clicks as I undo it.

Ronin draws in a breath.

I unzip his fly.

He lets out a moan.

I bite my lip, thinking about my next move just as Antoine

barks out, "OK, we're good."

It's like he does it on purpose.

Ronin sits up, grabs me under the ass, then lifts me up as he stands. He carries me up the stairs to his apartment and sets me down outside the door so he can punch in his key code, then whisks off my cape and tosses it to the floor and leads me down to the shower.

"I'm having déjà vu. How about you?"

He winks back at me. "Give it a minute. This will be nothing like this morning."

And it's not.

Ronin finishes what I started downstairs, his pants dropping to the tiled floor. He pushes some buttons on the shower control panel on the wall and brings up his favorite setting. Steam and drizzle.

When we shower together, it's like being on a tropical island.

The bucket and sponge are waiting, ready for Ronin to wash me off. He swishes the sponge in the bucket and then takes my left arm and drags the sponge down in one long swipe. My head tips back as I open my mouth to suck in a breath. Holy shit, this is just my arm!

He does the other arm, then bends down to caress my legs. "Open them a little, Gidge."

I am immediately wet right where he wants me to open up. But I do as I'm told.

He slides the sponge along the inside of my thigh, then up against my slit, parting it slightly, just enough to make me gasp. When I look down, he's smiling up.

He repeats this motion several times and each time I am so close, but just as I'm about to let it go, he pulls back, relieving the pressure. He doesn't let me come, but instead finishes my legs and moves on to my back. The sponge slides down the middle of my spine, then across my ass, and right between my legs. My clit practically has its own heartbeat right now.

When my back is clean to his satisfaction he turns me around and starts with my stomach, massaging little circles around my belly button, then sweeping down between my legs, just enough to remind me that I'm ready.

He drops the sponge in the bucket, swishes his hand around a little in the solution, then removes the paint from my breasts with his fingertips.

When all the paint has been cleaned, he repeats every single motion with the soap and by the time he's rinsing me with the detachable shower head, I'm about to explode all over him.

It's only then, when the paint is all gone and my body is soft and sweet-smelling, that he presses himself up against me. He's been hard the entire time but when he grinds against my hips, his hands on my ass to guide me along with his motions, he is more than hard. He is solid and thick.

"I love you."

My eyes search his as I take this all in. "I'm not sure what I feel, Ronin, but I really want to say that back to you."

He slides his hand behind my neck and laces his fingers into my wet hair. "So say it."

"I love you, too."

His kiss is immediate, almost before I'm finished uttering the words he was looking for. His mouth opens and I flick my tongue against his. He devours my mouth and for a few minutes we are breathless, moaning, and grasping for one another's most sensual parts. Then he draws back and leads me out of the shower, punching buttons on the control panel to turn it off as we walk by.

I'm still dripping wet when Ronin sweeps me off my feet and sets me down on the bed. He gently lifts my legs up and pushes my thighs apart, then delves down and devours me again.

I'm writhing in seconds, my back arching, my hands fisting the sheets. He pushes my thighs higher, exposing me further, and then sucks gently.

My moans are louder now and I squirm as the feeling becomes too intense.

He slips a finger inside me, sliding back and forth gently at first, then pumping harder as his thumb and tongue swirl against my nub.

I lose it.

I come hard against his mouth, my hands fisting his hair. He waits, his tongue dipping down as I continue to pulsate from the explosion of sensations. When I'm done he scoots up towards me, his thick erection in his hand, ready to enter.

But I push him back. "Not this time, Larue. My turn. Lie back."

He laughs. "It's not a *quid pro quo*, Gidget."

"I know." I've resisted giving him oral, I have bad memories of it from my ex. But I push that thought away and concentrate on the beautiful, caring man in front of me. He is a gentle lover. So, so gentle. "I want to, Ronin."

NINETEEN

RONIN

I didn't think it was possible to be any more turned on right now, but I am. Her words have turned me up a thousand decibels.

Rook watches me. "I want to, Ronin."

Her eyes are still half-mast from coming hard, her taste still on my tongue. I swallow because this girl—this girl makes me feel more than good. It's like every touch, every look, every sound that comes from her mouth is something sensual and perfect.

"Lie back," she says again.

My crooked grin makes her smile as I lie down next to her. She twists her body, pressing her breasts against my chest, then stretches up and kisses me, just little kisses at first, as if she's deciding if she likes the taste of herself. Then she straddles me and opens her mouth, her tongue done probing, ready for more.

Just as fast, she stops, her body sliding down, her chin rubbing against my stomach muscles as she descends. She plays with my hard-on for a second, then her tongue slides along the

MANIC

slit in my head and dips in for a taste.

Before I can even process how fucking good that feels, her mouth is desperate to wrap me up. She pumps again and again, sucking slightly, tonguing me as she pulls back, then massaging me with her lips as she descends down my shaft.

I give up.

The breath comes out of me in a soft rush as I relax back into the pillows and enjoy her. Fully enjoy her and everything she's doing right now. My whole body is on fire for this girl, my arms ache to flip her over and take her from behind, make her scream my name over and over again.

But I calm myself and suck in a breath between my teeth as I try to maintain control. I moan as the hot air of her laugh tickles the tip of my cock.

"Gidge," I say in a throaty whisper. My hands go to her head, pushing her slightly, compounding her rhythm as she evokes so much more in me than just a desire to come.

"Gidge," I repeat. "Climb on, baby."

She continues with her pumping and sucking but I'm not about to come this way. I sit up and toss her over on the bed next to me, then crawl up between her legs.

She's laughing at me.

"What's funny, Gidget?"

"You love me."

I laugh back. "I do, and I'm going to show you just how much every chance I get." I push her thighs open wider and flick my cock against her swollen clit a few times, back and forth, making her moan. She likes that.

I slide inside when she's in mid-gasp. She's so wet, so ready for me again. I ease in and out, slowly, then harder. Slow pumps become short thrusts, and then deep, penetrating, plunging assaults. Her back arches and her fingernails dig into my shoulders.

This is her signal. Her signal that she's gonna come and there's no way to avoid it.

At least that's what I think it says to her. But to me it says, *Do something spectacular right fucking now, Ronin, and I will make the most amazing noises for you.*

I reach down and play with her, slip between her folds and then sweep up to her clit and twirl my thumb, pushing it around gently in little circles.

She screams this time.

And I can't help it, this girl just does it for me. I lean down and growl into her neck as I come with her.

We fall asleep like this, me clutching her around the waist, her legs twined around mine in a way that makes me feel both wanted and whole. I wake once when she gets up to use the bathroom. But as soon as she returns to my bed I tug her ass up against me and fondle her breasts until we drift off again.

When we wake it's late afternoon. "Hey," I say, squeezing her breast a little. "Wake up, let's not waste the day."

She moans and turns away and I just have to smile. I've never met a girl who sleeps so soundly. She's not a naturally early riser and she's not easy to wake. Ever.

"Rook." I try again. This time I breathe into her ear and her shoulder draws up against my face.

She growls at me.

"Come on, I have plans for us."

"What plans?" she moans.

"Bike ride to the mountains."

"I don't wanna go to Black Hawk, I can't even gamble or drink. It's boring."

MANIC

"Not gambling, Rook. A ride up to Lookout Mountain. Come on, it's romantic. Besides, it's good practice for the road trip to Sturgis."

She turns. "I thought we were taking an RV up there?"

"We are, but you can't ride into Sturgis in an RV, Gidge." I laugh as I picture Spence RV'ing into Sturgis. "Spencer would be laughed out of town. He said he's working on your bike too, says it's real nice."

"When you'd talk about that? He never said anything to me."

I shrug. "I talked to him last night after you hung up on me."

She reaches out and pokes me in the arm with her fingernail. "You were checking up on me."

"Of course I was. That's my job."

She tilts her head and gives me a dirty look.

"It's not weird, Rook. It's normal. That's what boyfriends do for their girlfriends. This fear you have is unreasonable, ya know."

"I know," she pouts. "But I can't help it. When you say stuff like that it scares me. It feels invasive."

I lie back down and pull her close. The bike ride can wait. "It's not, though. It's normal."

"I don't like people talking about me, it bugs me." She stops and turns her head to look me in the eye. "It really bugs me."

"Well, you're not gonna be able to avoid it, Rook. Your face and body will be all over the world soon. You're in a reality show, you're on book covers in Japan, and a half a million people are gonna be talking all about you at the rally."

She wrinkles her nose at this.

"So I think it's OK if I ask Spencer what's going on. I'm still not sure what to think about what you said last night, about being turned on. I mean, I get it. I've been there. I get turned on too. But I've never had to talk about it with a girlfriend because the only other model I dated who was working with us at the time was Mardee. And I already told you, I was not all that nice to her. I never got jealous over her jobs."

Rook leans over and kisses me softly on the lips. "Sorry,"

she whispers into my mouth. "I just wanted to be honest. I just wanted you to tell me what it means. I want *you*, Ronin. Not Spencer. Not Billy. You."

"Yeah, well, I hate to disappoint you, but I'm not sure what it means."

"See, that's why Billy was so helpful. He told me it means nothing." She throws her hands out a little to illustrate her point. "He said he's always turned on, that's what Antoine wants and expects. But that it's meaningless. Even when he sleeps with the girl after, he says. It's meaningless."

"Huh." Billy's a fucking whore. The absolute last guy I want giving my girlfriend advice on what is and isn't normal in an erotic photo shoot. "You wanna do the bike ride?"

"Yeah, it sounds fun. Besides, I think I need to get out of this place for a while. I never go anywhere. I might need to buy a car."

"Why?"

She shoots me a dirty look.

"No, I mean, why *buy* one? I have two cars I never use. Just take one when you need it." Her silence tells me she's got a problem with this. "Rook, I swear, if you say something stupid like *I need my own car so you can't control me,* I'll handcuff you to the bed and show you what domination really looks like."

Her whole face screws up in disgust. "Don't joke. You know that's never gonna happen, right?"

"Yeah, I figured. But that doesn't mean I can't picture you like that. Your bottom bright pink from being spanked." She blushes and I am immediately hard. "Sounds fun, doesn't it?"

She doesn't answer that either way.

Progress.

TWENTY

ROOK

The evening with Ronin passes much too quickly. And he was right, as usual. Lookout Mountain has an amazing view of Denver. It's not even that far away, it barely took us thirty minutes to get to the freeway exit, but the winding road that climbs up the side of the mountain—foothill, Ronin corrects me, he scoffs at me when I call these rolling hills mountains—takes a whole lot longer. But I don't mind. I enjoy the vibrations of the bike beneath me. I press my cheek up against Ronin's leather jacket and gaze out at my new hometown as dusk takes over.

By the time we get to a little pull-out along the road, it's almost dark and the city lights down below are twinkling.

Ronin and I both look the part tonight. Matching leather jackets, courtesy of the Chaput closet, faded jeans, and black biker boots. My hair is in braids to keep it under control, and Ronin has one of those WWII helmet knock-offs for protection, but I'm wearing a proper one with the full face guard.

When I'm no longer pressed hard against Ronin's heat, I

MANIC

notice the chill. It's almost always pleasant down in Denver at night, but we're a couple thousand feet higher now, so the temperature dips as soon as the sun disappears over the peaks.

We don't stay long. I know enough about bikes to understand what a ride is and what it isn't. It's not a way to get somewhere, it's about enjoying the journey.

It's fitting for me, really. The journey is the only thing that counts because once you reach your destination, there's always somewhere else to go. Another journey to take.

Life is like that too.

I took a journey when I left Chicago. I struggled with homelessness and hunger. I feared for my safety and eventually, that journey ended with Antoine, Elise, and Ronin.

And now I'm on a new journey. I'm not sure where I'm going just yet. Maybe college. Maybe somewhere else.

Maybe marriage—eventually.

I know that's what Ronin wants, he's not kept it a secret about how much he wants a family. And I'm starting to think about what that means for me. I'm not on board yet, so I don't ponder it too seriously. But I watched Antoine and Elise when we were up at Granby Lake and it's nice what they have. They know each other so well and they're still very much in love.

I'd like that, too.

Someday.

But I'm only nineteen. It's just way too soon to think about forever. I like Ronin. Might even love him. I think he might be the one for me. But my life just started. I just got here. I'm not ready for the things he wants. Maybe I'll never be ready for kids. I'm not even sure about that.

I sigh into Ronin's back as he turns into the parking garage below the studio. We stopped at an Italian place in Golden to eat, and my day is finally catching up with me because I'm dead-ass tired.

I hand my helmet to Ronin and he locks everything up in the garage lockers, and then we take the elevator up instead of the stairs.

He knows I'm tired.

I like this about him. He made an effort to understand me after I told him what happened in Chicago. He pays very close attention to me. And I like that.

Most of the time, anyway. Tonight is one of those times.

When we get to the studio I try to walk up the stairs to his place, but he tugs my hand over to the terrace.

"Awww," I moan.

"Sorry, Gidge," he whispers into my ear as he opens the door. "But we have time for a swing, if you want."

"I do." God, can he be any more perfect? We walk over to the cherry trees and I plop down on the swing as he takes his position behind. He pushes me and my whole experience here at Chaput Studios comes rushing back with the wind as it whips my hair around.

"So, opinions on Ford. You guys getting along better yet?"

"I guess. He's OK."

"How about Spencer?"

I twist around as the swing goes back so I can catch a glimpse of Ronin behind me. "He's funny."

Ronin laughs. "Yeah, he is. He's not a bad guy."

"Is Ford?"

"I hate Ford. Really, seriously, hate his fucking guts."

I'm not surprised. But I am surprised he told me that. Ronin is a professional and the relationship we have with Ford right now is business. Which means what he said was unprofessional.

"Wanna tell me about it?"

"Nah, he's not worth it." Ronin stops the swing and takes my hand so we can walk back to my apartment. "Ford said they want you up on Fort Collins this weekend to film you hanging out with Spencer."

"Oh, that sucks. I figured I'd have the weekend off."

"Yeah, me too. But Ford—never mind."

He stops. Maybe because we're at my door or maybe because

MANIC

he realizes he's not supposed to talk shit about a client.

Either way, I don't push it. "Are you coming up there with me?"

He cups my face in his hands and kisses me tenderly on the lips. Just a small, slow kiss with no tongue. "I wouldn't miss it, Gidget. We'll ride up in the truck after breakfast."

I kiss him back a little more forcefully.

He laughs and pulls back. "I'd love to take you in there right now and make love to you, Rook. But I have some work to do and want to call and check on Clare before bed. So I'll come by in the morning, OK?"

"OK," I say, nodding.

He leans in and kisses me softly again. All the urgency of our earlier tryst is gone and now it's just easy and long. I kiss him back and then lean my head on his shoulder. "I love you," I whisper.

His fingers thread through my hair and he kisses me again, only this time it's on the top of my head. A protective, emotional kiss. "I'm so in love with you, Rook. So fucking in love with you, it scares me."

"But it's a good scary, right?"

He chuckles. "Yes, definitely a good scary." He turns, holding my hand until the last possible second, our fingers not quite willing to let go, and then he slips away and goes back to the studio.

I go inside and plop down on my couch and flip on the TV and channel-surf for a while. It's been a long day, but a good one. It's still pretty confusing. I'm not sure what to make of my job. I'm not sure if getting painted up naked and kissing other guys as part of work is cheating or not. If I was on Ronin's end of things I'd certainly be jealous. And I'm sure he is, but he's got a lot of self-control.

He deserves lots and lots of points for that.

And I'm pretty sure he's pissed off about Ford and Spencer making me go up to the bike shop this weekend, but he handled that well, too. We haven't had time to talk about the next job Spencer wants to offer me, but I'm open to considering it. It's not modeling, and that's good. I don't want to model any more. I've had enough. This contract will pay me a lot of money and I bet if we really do get a whole season of shows on the Biker Channel that will pay pretty well too. Granted, the show is about Spencer and his bikes and body painting, but if I wasn't an important part of that I wouldn't be Spencer's first choice. Plus, by the time that contract comes up I'll sorta be famous all on my own. They'll have to offer me something nice, or else why would I take the job?

They don't know how much I hate this naked stuff. In fact, I should stop whining about it so they think I *want* to take another job, that way I'll have a better chance at negotiating more money if I do get the contract. I could just tell them how much other offers would pay and make them match it.

I smile at this and then turn the TV off, change into some shorts and a t-shirt, and slide into bed.

Exhausted, but not scared.

TWENTY-ONE

ROOK

I'm ready right at five this morning but Ford never comes to my door. I can see him out on the terrace, sitting backwards at one of the stone picnic tables on the side of the building, not facing me. He's just kickin' it, like he's got all the time in the world. I watch him for a couple minutes to see what he does if I don't come out. He never checks his watch or even hints that he's waiting for me. Just sits, his arms resting comfortably on the table, his legs stretched out in front of him.

I open my door and he looks over at me and then gets to his feet. "I was beginning to wonder."

"Wonder what?" I ask as I walk over to him.

"If you would show up or blow me off because you have Ronin to run interference now."

"Hey, a deal's a deal, right? And besides, I was watching you for like five minutes and you never once looked like you cared if I came or not."

"I'm not forcing you to come."

MANIC

"Well, technically, Ford, you are. You asked for this deal and I agreed."

"Yes, but do you really think I'd put the cameras back in if you refused to run with me?"

"Yeah."

He looks over at me with a crooked grin on his face. "I wouldn't, Rook. So if you'd like to skip out, feel free."

I say nothing, just follow him over to the studio door. He holds it open for me, and we walk down the stairs and cross the street. We go to the upper level seats this time and Ford doesn't say a word. Just sets his watch, to time himself I guess, and takes off running up the stairs.

For some reason starting at the bottom and going up seems harder to me. When we run the lower stairs we start at the top and it feels different going down. I trudge up, walk over to the next set, then stomp back down. I'm not as winded as I was the first day, so by the time Ford stops to check his time and head back towards me, I've covered a significant number of rows. I watch Ford's expression as he runs towards me. It's flat. Well, no, not really flat. It's more like a grimace. Like he's determined or something.

When he gets near he stops to catch his breath, leaning over like he always does, like he's about to heave. "Why do you run like that, Ford?"

"Like what?" he asks, uprighting himself briefly, then bending over again. He's so sweaty it drips off his face and plops to the ground.

Surprisingly, this does not gross me out. "Like you're trying to catch someone."

He doesn't look up this time. "Maybe I'm running away from something?"

I shake my head at him. "No, I don't think so. You're not someone who runs away."

He smiles and straightens up, his breath back to normal now. Which means this guy is in awesome shape. Because if that was me, I'd be on the ground gasping like a fish on the beach for like an hour. "You're right. I'm not running away. I never look back, I only move forward."

"Interesting," I say before I even realize the words are coming out.

"What's interesting about it?" He moves forward towards me, his eyes locked on mine. When I back up I find the wall behind me. I press against it as Ford takes a few more steps towards me. "Are you a runner, Rook? Or a chaser?"

I swallow because he's very close now, only a few inches. He's as tall as Ronin, easy. So I have to turn my head up a little to match his gaze. "A runner," I whisper.

He places his palms against the wall on either side of my body, but he keeps those few inches between us. "Do you look back?"

I shake my head, still transfixed by his stare. "No," I say, gulping a little bit of air. "Or, at least I try not to."

He removes his hands and waves me towards the door that will lead inside to the breakfast burritos. "And how successful are you at moving forward right now?" he asks as we pass through the door and walk down the lobby hallway that curves around the stadium, following the smell of food.

"Well…" I let out a deep sigh. "I'd say average. I'm not dwelling, but I'm not over it yet, not completely, anyway."

He stops walking and grabs my hand. "Over what yet?"

I laugh it off a little and shake my hand free. "I've had a rough life, Ford. I'm new money."

"Ah," he says, like I just gave away a piece of vital information. "So that's why Ronin likes you so much. You *are* damaged."

"Hey, that's fucking rude. I'm not damaged. I had a problem, I took care of it, and now I *am* moving forward."

"Then you're a chaser, Rook. Own it, if that's what you are."

"I'm neither, Ford. Or, maybe I'm both at the moment. I'm not ashamed that I ran. It was the best decision I ever made."

"How did you get here?"

MANIC

"Where?"

"This moment in time. How did you end up *here*, inside Coors Field, running with me? Where did you grow up?"

It takes me back a minute because I'm so used to Ronin avoiding my past. I watch Ford's eyes as I consider if I'll answer him and he waits me out. Not making a move, not making a sound. Just calm. He exudes patience.

"Chicago," I finally say.

"OK, now tell me how you got *here*."

"I walked across the street with you."

He chuckles a little under his breath. "Did you fly? Drive?"

"Bus."

"Ahhh. That makes sense. So why Denver? What made you want to come to Denver of all places?"

"Well…" I go over to a table near the windows and Ford follows me. We sit across from each other, him facing the sun, and me with my back to it. "I was actually on my way to Vegas but I was sitting across the aisle from these boys going to Denver. And they were watching *South Park* on their tablet the entire ride." I stop to laugh because I love *South Park*. "And that stupid Cartman, he gets me very time, so I was eavesdropping, trying to listen for him to say one of his funny lines."

Ford's serious expression falters and he smiles with me.

"Anyway, they were talking about how those guys who made *South Park* went to the university in Boulder and since my dream has always been to go to film school, I figured it was a sign and maybe Denver was where I was supposed to end up, so I took a chance on fate and just… stepped off the bus."

I wait for Ford to say something but he just shakes his head and smiles.

"What?"

"I went to Boulder and majored in film."

"Hmmm. That's sorta weird."

He stares at me, his eyes bright as his mind takes this in. "Fate, you say?"

144

"Well, weird, at the very least."

"So you were compelled to get off a bus in Denver because of *South Park* and the CU Boulder film department?"

"Yeah, that's how it happened. I had nothing to lose, ya know? So why not? Why not take a chance here?" I shrug. "It seems to be working out OK."

Ford stands and I stand with him. "Thank you for telling me that, Rook. It's a great story."

"No problem. I'm hungry now, can we eat?"

He smiles and we start walking down the corridor towards the smell of food and when we get close to it Ford guides me over to a table with his hand on my back. I take a seat but he stays standing. "I'll get your food. Stay here."

I sigh. Ronin would probably not like me talking to Ford about personal things, but Ford said Ronin likes damaged girls. No, correction—*young*, damaged girls. And that's me for sure. And I can't help myself, I feel the need to know more about this. If I'm just another project to Ronin, I'd like to figure that out sooner rather than later. I like him a whole lot and I don't want to get hurt.

Ford comes back and hands me my burrito and OJ, then takes a seat across from me and begins to chow down. I do the same and we are too busy chewing to talk for a while. He finishes before me, because he's a guy and every guy I've ever met has been a scarfer when it comes to food. He balls up the foil burrito wrapper and finishes off his juice and then starts with the questions.

"How long has it been?" he asks. "Since you ran?"

I think back and count the weeks. "About three months," I finally say with my mouth full.

"How long have you known Ronin?"

"About a month." I stay quiet, waiting for his next question, but he looks away, like he's thinking about my answer. "Why?" I finally ask.

"I'm just trying to figure out what it means that he claimed you."

That word almost makes me choke. "He didn't *claim* me, Ford. We're dating. That's it."

"Huh." He looks over at me now. "How many men, Rook? Not to get personal, but I'm just curious. How many men have you been with?"

"What's that got to do with anything?"

"Because you come off as very, *very* inexperienced. That's why. It makes you seem far younger than you really are."

I snort. "OK, I guess you're the expert in sexual experience, then?" I just shake my head at him. I'm not answering that question. It sorta pisses me off, in fact. I wrap my burrito back up in the foil and get up and walk away.

He catches up with me as I'm going down the stairs.

"Too personal?"

"Yeah, Ford. I'm sorry I told you that story now. You're gonna do something dirty with it, I can tell." I stop and look at him. My face feels so hot I wonder if I'll start crying. "Just leave me alone." I start to walk off but he grabs my arm firmly and doesn't let go, even when I try to jerk away.

"Wait. I'm not trying to upset you, Rook."

I whirl around. "Like hell you're not! And you're doing a good job of it too, because I like Ronin, OK? I like him and you've told me twice now that I'm nothing to him aside from some sort of project. That he's only interested in me because he has a sick hero complex. And it makes me feel…"

Jesus Christ, Rook. Why are you telling this guy about your feelings? Get a grip.

I yank my arm away and continue down the stairs.

Ford follows me but stays a few steps behind, then catches up and holds the door when I throw it open and go out to the parking lot.

"Makes you feel what, Rook? Used?"

I stop again. "Yeah, OK? You make me feel like he's using me. And he's not, you are! You're using me to mess things up between us and..."

"And what?"

I hold that in and keep walking.

"And keep you for myself? Is that what you think, Rook?"

"No, Ford. That's not what I think."

"Then your instincts are off, because that's exactly what I'm doing."

I stop again. "Holy shit! You are such an asshole!"

And then he smiles. And it's not a smile I've ever seen on him before. It's like all his other smiles were fake and I'm just now seeing real happiness on his face for the first time.

It disarms me. Completely. And he knows it because he moves closer to me, not touching me, but very close. It makes me uncomfortable and I look around, feeling guilty. There's no one else in the parking lot. There are a lot of cars on the street, but we're still a good hundred yards from the street.

"I won't touch you, Rook, don't worry," he whispers. "I'm not a runner and I'm not a cheater, either. Life is long, you are young, and I'm very, *very* patient."

My expression hardens, all traces of insecurities disappear in an instant and I look him in the eyes. "I'm not worried, Ford. Because if you touch me, I'll knee you in the balls so hard it'll be weeks before you can run stadiums again."

TWENTY-TWO

ROOK

Ronin is waiting for me in the garden apartment when I get back. He's kicking back on the couch watching some news channel. "Hey," I say as I walk through the door.

He throws his hands wide. "Where the hell did you go?"

"I run stadiums with Ford in the mornings now, remember? It's a deal we made to get the cameras out of my bedroom."

"Stadiums." He thinks about this for a second. "Why?"

I huff out a breath. "I just told you to keep—"

"No, why *running*?"

"Well, *I* don't run," I snort. "I mope, shuffle practically. But Ford runs like a maniac. Like he's chasing—" I stop. Because Ronin has a weird look on his face. "Um, I'm not sure what's going on with you guys, you and Spencer and Ford, but you all could use a lesson in poker faces. That's all I'm saying. Because obviously there is something you three are not telling me and it's getting weird."

He turns away from me, hiding.

MANIC

"Ronin," I say, sitting down next to him. "What's the deal? Is something wrong?"

He looks back to me and sighs. "No, nothing's wrong. It's just we have a very complicated history and—"

I wait a few seconds, but he turns away again, like he needs a moment to think of what to say. "And what?" I prod.

"This whole project is a bad idea. I don't know what Spencer was thinking."

"Because you and Ford don't get along?"

For a second I think he's about to tell me something really important. Like he's got words just aching to get out. But then his expression hardens. "What do you and Ford talk about? When you run together?"

Oh shit! Is he psychic or something? I suddenly feel guilty, even though I did nothing wrong. I'm not responsible for Ford's words. I walked away, threatened him even. "Nothing, really. He just said that I was too young to do this contract, it's probably a very big mistake, and he's not gonna be the one responsible if things turn out bad."

Ronin just stares at me.

"He says there's something wrong with me"—I leave out the part where he said Ronin only likes broken girls that he can try to save—"and exercise will help me cope or some shit like that."

Ronin is absolutely still and quiet, but I only have to watch his eyes to see that his mind is going crazy on the inside.

"Ronin?"

He lets out a long breath. "Stay away from him, Rook. No more running."

"Why?"

"Does it matter why?" He gives me a sideways glance. "If I tell you to stay away from him, isn't that good enough?"

I laugh. "No, it's not. I'm not your pet, Ronin. Maybe I'll run with him tomorrow and maybe I won't but either way, I won't be making that decision based on your orders."

"Since when is asking my girlfriend not to spend time with a guy I don't trust out of bounds?"

He's right, of course. Ford just made a move on me. Maybe not in a normal way, but that was definitely a move. "Ronin, I'm not a piece of property, OK? If you've got information about him that I should know, or you think he's gonna hurt me—"

"Don't be dramatic, Rook. He's not going to *hurt* you."

"Oh! Me? I'm not the drama queen here, Ronin. That's you and Ford." I get up and walk outside, not really sure where I'm going, but fuck him. I knew it. I knew as soon as I let him have some control he'd start this caveman shit with me. And I've been there. I see the signs very clearly and right now they're flashing bright red just so I can't miss them. I walk over to the cherry tree swing and then the screen door slaps closed behind me and Ronin follows me over.

I settle in the seat and he's already apologizing as he walks.

"I'm sorry, Rook. OK? I don't mean to set you off like that—"

"Set me off like what? I walked out the door calmly, I'd hardly call that *setting me off*."

He stops in front of me and my feet scuff against the grass as I wait for him to answer. "You're a runner, Rook. You learned that if you've got problems you can make them go away by walking out. Or getting on a bus and just disappearing. So you walking out of our conversation *was* the perfect example of you being set off."

I laugh. "Sorry, my mistake. I didn't realize marketing degrees required psychology classes as well."

He walks over to me and takes my hand. "OK, just answer me one question then. What part of me asking you to stay away from Ford bothers you? Why do you care?"

"You didn't give me a good reason. If you want me to ignore him then tell me why."

"I—" His phone buzzes and he reaches into his pocket to check the text, saying nothing for several seconds. Then he texts back and turns to me. "Fuck. I have to go back up to Steamboat."

"What? Why?"

MANIC

"Clare escaped."

Fucking Clare. It's like she's doing this shit on purpose.

"They found her in the nearby woods, so she's OK. But Elise says she's asking for me and the doctors are so pissed off right now, they might kick her out. I'll just stay one night, I'll be back tomorrow, OK?"

"Just like that? Clare's in trouble so you drop everything, drop *me*, to go save *her*?"

He steps forward, takes my hand, and pulls me up off the swing. "Rook, if you were the one who needed help I'd drop everything for you, too."

"But I'm good now, right? I don't need help. Now Clare needs you."

He shrugs. "That sounds like a loaded question, but I'm not sure what you're getting at, so yeah. That's about it. You know where the cars keys are, Gidge. Help yourself to the cars, or whatever else you need, OK?" He drops my hand and turns to leave.

"Wait! Why can't I come with you?"

He turns and gives me a weird look. "It's not a vacation. She's addicted to heroin. She doesn't even know you. She's sick and she doesn't want to see anyone but us. "

"You, you mean, right? Because Antoine and Elise are already there. So she just wants to see *you*."

He leans down and kisses me on the cheek. The fucking *cheek*. "I'll be back tomorrow morning and we'll drive up to Fort Collins together, OK?"

And he turns and walks away.

I swear, I'm so stunned I can't even move. I don't even know how long I sit there out on the swing before I go lie down under the tree. And after that, I have no idea how long I lie there alone, staring up into the canopy of leaves and branches, before Ford is suddenly standing next to me.

"What?" I ask.

"There's a camera in the trees."

"So you heard all that."

"Just agree with him, Rook. I don't care if you ignore me. Don't fight over something so stupid."

I sit up and shield my eyes from the sun so I can see his face. "He thinks you're some creeper, Ford. And you're OK with that assumption?"

He shrugs. "Yes."

And then he turns and walks off. His steps even and emotionless as he crosses the terrace and makes his way inside.

I laugh a little under my breath. This contract was a mistake, but fuck it. I'm making bank right now. When this is over I'll have enough to go to California if I want. Just move to LA and fight for my dream. Because in the last twenty-four hours I've thought about breaking up with Ronin twice and that's not a good sign as far as potential long-term relationships go.

TWENTY-THREE

ROOK

Ford is sitting outside promptly at five minutes to five the next morning.

For half a second I consider not going. But I'm already dressed in the stupid athletic shorts and tight-ass top. As soon as I go out he stands and walks to the studio door and holds it open for me. "You surprise me, Rook," he says matter-of-factly as I walk through, mumbling out a *thank you*.

"Why? Because I keep my promises?"

"No, because even though you're smart and capable of a whole lot more than posing naked and accepting your fate as Ronin's project, you choose this life and let people walk all over you."

I snort but I do not even dignify that with a response. Fuck him. He says nothing else the entire walk over and when we get inside he waits for me to choose top or bottom stairs.

I head through the door that leads to the bottom seats because I prefer to start at the top and go down. As soon as we

MANIC

get inside the stadium he takes off and leaves me there. I watch him as I shuffle down my section of stairs. He starts off at a faster pace than usual, like he's turning it up a notch. I shake myself out of this fog Ford has draped over me and concentrate on my own workout. It's not as difficult as it was the first day and when I get to the bottom and start to climb the next section I make a little bit of effort.

Just a little.

I decide to see how fast I can go and for how long, so I take off booking it up the stairs. At first it feels good to exert myself like this because I've been angry since yesterday morning and I need to burn it off. I run hard all the way up to the top, then dash down the aisle to the next set of stairs and go down as fast as I can and repeat the mad dash over to the next set. I climb again, fully exerting myself, but soon my thighs are burning and about three-quarters of the way up I have to slow down because they are on fire. I stop and look behind me and let off a little smile. Maybe I'm a total stadium-running loser compared to Ford, but this is a challenging exercise and I didn't do too bad.

I look over to find Ford and to my surprise he's not running. He's watching me. I walk up the remaining steps and he starts heading my direction.

My stomach flips a little at this change-up in our routine.

"What are you doing?" I ask when he gets close enough so I don't have to yell.

"You're ready now?"

"Ready for what?"

"To work."

I'm tired of his cryptic messages. "Whatever, Ford. I just wanted to see how fast I could go for how long. Don't get excited, I'm not about to morph into some health nut. I come here because we made a deal. If you want the deal to be over, stop fucking showing up outside my apartment at five AM. It's real simple. If you're not there, I don't go." He smiles that hidden smile again, and it confuses me for a second. Why is he smiling now? "Are we done for today or what?"

"Do you want to be done?"

"It's up to you, Ford."

"No, Rook, it's up to you. I'm not done, but you're free to go if you wish."

More psychology bullshit from him. "Why are you so weird? What kind of game are you playing with me?"

"Just run the stadiums, Rook. Is that what you want me to tell you? Give you orders? Are you waiting for orders?"

Am I?

I turn and walk away.

Because I might be. I might actually be waiting for him to tell me what to do. It makes me sick when I think about it.

A hand grasps my upper arm and I whirl around.

"OK, wait," Ford says as he looks down at me. "Just answer this, Rook. Do you want to come here with me in the mornings?"

Silence from me.

"Well? It's either yes or no."

I laugh at that. Because it's not that easy. If I say yes and mean it, then I'd have to start asking myself a whole bunch of other questions. If I say no, well, that's just a lie. Because the fact is, I do want to come here with him. I sorta like it. I like the fact that he's outside every morning. He's weirdly reliable. And strangely persistent. "Yes."

He smiles that smile again and my whole stomach flutters. "OK, so get busy then. If you're going to spend time here, don't waste it. Make it count."

And then he turns around and starts running again.

I turn as well and start down my set of stairs at a faster clip. Going down isn't easy at a run because the steps are not even, it's like you have to take two steps forward and then step down. It's an odd rhythm. My legs hurt when I get to the bottom, but not in the same way as when I go back up. I'm slower this time, my muscles more strained, but I have to admit, when I get to the top I feel pretty exhilarated. I continue this way, and with each set I

MANIC

get slower and slower. By the time Ford turns to head back my way I'm sitting down leaning up against the cinder-block wall.

He leans over and lets the sweat drip as he catches his breath.

"So you gonna tell me who you're chasing? Or are you the only one who gets to ask questions?" Two can play this game.

He straightens, just like he did yesterday, but instead of turning away he slides down the wall and sits next to me. "You have no idea who Ronin is, Rook."

Everything inside me does a little flip. "What?"

"It's not a disparaging remark. Just a fact."

"But you do? That's what you're saying?"

"I do," he says matter-of-factly. "I've watched him in some very stressful situations, and he's seen me under the same circumstances. We know each other well."

"So when he tells me you're fucked in the head, then that's just as true as you telling me he's only using me to play out his hero fantasy."

That smile again. I have to look away and wait for his answer.

"My father was a famous psychiatrist. I was a weird kid, I liked reading and computers and I wanted to be like my dad, so I read all his books on human behavior and psychology and I used to freak people out in school by diagnosing them with clinical disorders and fucking with their school records online."

He laughs and when I look over at him I can't help myself, I smile at his huge grin.

It's the first personal thing he's ever told me. "Are you using that psych bullshit on me right now? By confiding in me with this sincere admission of childhood nerdiness?"

He grins again and this time his smile lights up his brown eyes. "You know, you're very smart. You don't belong here. And I might've come across a little strange back in school, so I can't blame Ronin for his opinion, plus I pulled a fucked-up prank on him once. It was stupid and childish, and not something he'd forget easily. But I'm not trying to make your life difficult, Rook. I'm just trying to make you stronger."

"So I won't need Ronin."

He turns to look at me and now the smile is gone. My stomach knots up as I meet his gaze. "Yes. That's why. I have a disadvantage here because I don't want people to need me like Ronin does. I don't want to slow down for someone, Rook. I want someone to keep up with me."

"But that's selfish."

"Why?"

"Because if you like someone you should want to help them."

"I am helping you."

I roll my eyes at him. "Not me, specifically. I just think that if you like someone you'd be willing to give up a little piece of yourself to keep them. If you really liked someone, you'd be OK with slowing down."

"All right, then why did you insist on taking this contract when Ronin was against it? Why not give up that choice to please Ronin?"

"Because I like making my own choices, Ford. So if I want to model nude for a butt-load of money, so what? I'm allowed to do that and it's no one's business but mine. "

"Just because you *can* make that choice doesn't mean you *should*. There's a big difference between being in control of your future and making bad decisions."

I shrug. "So?" But I laugh a little because I sound like a two-year-old.

"OK," he sighs. "Would you like my childhood psycho-babble interpretation of what you're doing right now?"

I swallow. Do I? Not really, but this conversation with Ford is oddly compelling. "Go for it."

"You resist Ronin's advice because you're not ready for it yet. But at the same time you need someone slow and controlling very badly right now. Just like I need someone free and fast. Whatever it was that happened to you, you're looking for someone to make it better, but for some reason you're having a hard time admitting that to yourself. So you're in this weird

MANIC

in-between stage that justifies mistakes in the name of freedom. And whatever it is you're trying to fix, I'd just like to say Ronin's not the answer. Because there's only one person who can fix that mistake you made, Rook."

"Me?" I ask in a whisper as I watch his eyes.

"You," he answers softly. "I'm not trying to fix you, I'm just trying to give you the tools to fix yourself."

"I actually already knew all that stuff, Ford. And besides, I've already saved myself."

He chuckles under his breath. "Not quite, Rook. You're like Clare right now. In treatment but resisting. It's a long road to recovery."

He gets up and offers me his hand. I accept it and he pulls me to my feet. We skip breakfast and walk back across the street and despite the very personal nature of our conversation today, we part ways in silence when he gets to his car.

Ford is one weird guy.

I go home and climb back into bed, tired and relaxed from the morning exercise.

TWENTY-FOUR

ROOK

"Hey," Ronin whispers in my ear as he settles against my body later. "You awake?"

I roll over and look at him. "Yeah, how's Clare?"

He sucks in a long breath. "She's iffy."

"She can't kick the heroin? Or what? I don't understand what's going on."

"It's not an easy habit to kick, Gidge. It's got something to do with brain chemistry, she thinks she's dying but it's the withdrawal symptoms. We're just trying to get her over the worst of it." He pulls me into his chest. "What'd you do while I was gone?"

"Ran with Ford, slept, moped." I look up at him and smile. "Waited for you to come back."

"How is Ford?"

"He's weird, Ronin. He's a weird guy."

His whole body stiffens underneath me for a second, then relaxes. "What'd he say?" He sounds worried.

I sit up and look down at him. "He said I like being told what to do."

This makes Ronin pull away. "What?"

"Yeah, some crap about waiting for orders."

"That guy is unbelievable."

"Why?"

"Never mind, Gidge. But if you're interested in taking orders, then take mine. Stay away from him. He's not a nice guy."

I say nothing.

"Let me guess, he said the same thing about me?"

"Yeah, sorta. He said you like broken girls so you can fix them. Do you think I'm broken?"

He nuzzles into my neck. "You're so strong, Rook. You're the farthest thing from broken I've ever seen. Please stop running with him. He's a mind-fuck. He does it on purpose. His father was some big-shot psychiatrist, just as nasty as Ford before he died. Ford is one fucked-up dude. And you wanna know why I hate his fucking guts? Because when I was in the tenth grade and he was a senior, he looked up the police report about my father, made copies of it, and then plastered it all over school. Antoine went ballistic, but Ford's father donated a bunch of money to the school and nothing ever happened to him. He's a total asshole."

But this revelation has lost its shock value because Ford preemptively confessed all this. "Then why do this project, Ronin?"

"Antoine and Elise wanted the contract and I'm only one-third partner. They're socking money away like crazy for something they're not sharing with me. So there was nothing I could do. It's not Ford's money, anyway, it's the Biker Channel people. But enough about Ford. I missed you and I'm sorry I just walked off like that. Antoine's desperate to make things right with Clare. This is our last chance, you know? She's just a total mess."

I snuggle into him. I really want to love Ronin and I'm not sure Ford knows what he's talking about. He hasn't seen Ronin in a long time. So even if Ronin used to be looking for a girl to save, that doesn't mean he's still like that now.

His hands slide up my t-shirt and I gasp as he pokes my ribs. "What," he asks innocently, "is the problem, ma'am?"

I twist and squirm as he continues to poke me, giggling as I try and get away from his tickling touch.

"Ma'am, are you resisting arrest?" He leans down to sniff me. "Have you been drinking? I might have to taste you to find out." He kisses me, just a little tease to see if I'm interested. My mouth opens and our tongues tangle and tumble together.

Oh, I am so interested.

He nuzzles into my neck, then bites my earlobe gently and kisses his way down my throat, cups one breast while he sucks gently on the other.

"Wait! I have to confess something."

"Ma'am, I'm gonna have to ask you to remain silent." He tips his head up as he slides down the bed then positions himself between my legs.

"But I have a confession."

He looks up at me and grins. "I'll use it against you, ya know."

"I understand."

"OK, confess."

"I'm hiding drugs," I say with a stupid grin.

"Really?" His eyebrows waggle at me.

I bust out a laugh and nod. "Yes."

His hands go for my shorts. "I'm gonna have to strip-search you then. Sorry, ma'am. Just following procedures." He pulls down my shorts, taking my panties at the same time. "Take off your shirt, Rook." He breaks character and it comes out as a command.

But it's pretty hot the way he says it so I sit up and pull my t-shirt over my head. His gaze falls to my breasts and then he leans forward and sucks on my nipple again, using his fingertips and tongue at the same time to make it bunch up and get hard.

"I love that," he says as he drags himself back down my body, sitting up slightly to grab my legs under the knees and push them forward. His tongue teases little circles around my nub and then dips inside me, twisting and tasting. His hands slide up my ribcage and he palms both breasts, hard, then softly. My hands go to his hair and I fist it and push his mouth into me. His hot breath on my most tender parts is about to push me over the edge.

He pulls back just as the intensity starts to build and I moan. He slides back up and kisses my mouth. I draw my legs up and grind against his erection through his boxer briefs.

"Take those off," I say. If he can command, then so can I.

He grins and laces his fingers through my left hand. I'm just about to think that's totally sweet when he lifts it slowly over my head, gently lets go and wraps my palm around the wrought iron bars of the headboard. He repeats this exact same move with my other hand until both are above my head grasping hold of the bars.

"Stay still, Rook."

I know what he's doing and even though it sorta ticks me off that he's pulling this dominant shit with me, it also sorta turns me on. So I do stay still. I watch him as he gets up and rummages through my drawers until he comes up with a silk scarf.

"Ronin—"

"Shhh. Just quiet now," he says as he comes back over to the bed. "You're not being restrained, Rook. You wanna take it off, just take it off." He waits to see what I'll say. "OK?"

He's waiting for me to give him permission. I've modeled with him enough to know if he asks me a sexual question like that he wants an answer. "OK."

His grin is immediate. "Lift your head up a little." I do and he ties the scarf around my eyes. The scarf is yellow, so it's not dark. I think he did this on purpose because I know for a fact there are black scarves in that drawer. He picked a yellow one so while my sight will be restricted, it won't be dark.

When he joins me in bed he's missing his boxer briefs. He slides between my legs and I feel his firm erection against my thigh. My heart rate kicks up a few notches as the excitement begins to build.

I'm definitely turned on and that surprises me because I just handed him control. I suck in a sharp breath between my teeth as he starts with kisses. This time they are hard and desperate. My breathing gets all ragged and I push myself against him, rubbing a little. He enters me and we find our rhythm. There is nothing scary about this at all.

"Rook," he whispers into my neck. "I want you in my bed every night." He thrusts into me and I gasp and buckle my back, holding onto the iron bars so tight it almost hurts. He repeats that move over and over—our bodies hard and fast one moment, then still, or slow the next. He pulls out, almost completely out, then slides back inside me. And again, he varies the rhythm so just as I'm getting used to his motion, it changes and the new sensations demand my attention.

He leans down into my neck and lets out a steamy breath of desire. "It feels good to give in, doesn't it?"

"This feels good." I can feel his smile against my skin and I smile too. "But maybe next time I can blindfold you?"

"You wanna be on top, Gidge?"

He likes me on top and I like it too. "Yes, please."

He growls against my neck again. "You have nice manners, Miss Walsh. Now let go of the headboard." I do and before I know what's happening he flips us over and I'm straddling his waist. My hand goes up to the blindfold. "No," he says, stopping me with a firm grasp. "Leave it."

I obey, then lift up and wrap my palm around his thickness. We are both very ready. I guide him inside me and then let myself dip down. His hands are on my hips, encouraging me to move back and forth instead of up and down. This drives me crazy and he knows it.

"Come here, Gidge." He gently grabs my shoulders and pulls my upper body down on top of his muscular chest. "Stay right here." And then he takes over, alternating between thrusting and

MANIC

sliding me against him in just the right way so that my clit is throbbing with the friction. I draw my knees up a little so I can push myself against him.

"God, you feel so good, Rook." His hands are on my ass now, squeezing, and then he lifts up and gives me a small smack. Not enough to hurt but definitely enough to make me want more. The next time he does it I moan and increase my movement, lifting up and then slamming down on him. "Yeah, that's nice," he says and when the hand smacks down for the third time I explode.

I come so hard I can't stop the scream.

TWENTY_FIVE

ROOK

Fort Collins, or FoCo as Ronin likes to call it, is a about an hour's drive north of Denver. Spencer's shop is just northwest of the city outside a tiny town called Bellvue. It sits on a large piece of land that bucks up against the Cache La Pouder River and the shop is really a large barn behind a massive white farmhouse.

This place is totally cute.

Ford, being the asshole that he is, put a car cam in Ronin's truck for the ride up so we dutifully said next to nothing the entire time just to piss Ford off. Now that the crew is back I'm less enthusiastic about being chatty, so I let Ronin do all the talking. He's discussing things with Spencer and Team Rook is messing with the microphone when Ford walks over to me.

I do my best to ignore him, but it's not easy because he just stands there and waits out my silence.

"What?" I finally ask as I turn to look up at him.

He shakes his head at me. "Don't let him talk for you, Rook. Stop moping about the cameras and make decisions. This is your

MANIC

life they're discussing." And then he walks off.

He's right, I have to admit that. I should be over there talking about this. I walk over to Ronin and Spence and Ronin puts his arm around my waist and pulls me close as he continues talking. "Two places," Ronin says to Spencer. "That's it."

"Two places, what?" I ask.

"Four, Ronin. I need her to meet everyone on this trip so we get a good rapport going with the locals. I get that you don't want her doing the whole season, but she already signed a contract for the pilot, and the purpose of the pilot is to generate good footage so we get the whole season."

"What places?" I ask again.

"Spencer, she was contracted to do modeling, not be your errand girl. She's a *model*, not your bitch."

"What's going on?"

"Yeah, but the modeling included the reality show, so technically she is my bitch."

"Spencer—"

"Rook," Ronin says, a little exasperated. "Please, just let me manage the contractual stuff, OK?" He kisses me on the head and points over to the far end of the shop. "There's your bike, go check it out."

Hmph. I walk off. Should I be mad at that exchange? He's my manager, he's just doing his job. I look back for Team Rook to see if they've sorted the microphone yet, but they are still busy setting things up. I stop and check out the bike I chose last month when I was at Spencer's showroom and he painted my back up. It was just a plain bike back then, reminiscent of a classic Triumph with a flashy turquoise tank. Now it's all turquoise. The frame, the fenders, and even the long classic leather seat.

But the thing that really makes this bike stand out now is the logo. Every bike gets its own logo and my bike is called the Shrike Rook. It's so perfect I can hardly contain my glee! It's got a cool swirly feathered blackbird in the middle of a blood red circle and the letters are in a font most heavy metal bands could appreciate.

The girly feathers repeat on the fenders and are embroidered on the seat.

"It's nice, huh?" Ford asks.

"God, yes! He said he'd customize it a bit, but I never imagined he'd go to all this trouble. It's... *stunning*." I laugh a little and look over at him.

He's not even smiling.

"What?"

"That was underwhelming, Rook. You didn't even get them to look at you."

I let out a long breath. "Ford, he's my manager, that's his job. Now leave me alone."

"Rook!" Ronin barks at me from across the room. I can see Ford give me a look out of the corner of my eye but I ignore him.

"Yeah," I reply, turning to walk back over to Ronin.

He meets me halfway, throwing a pissed-off look at Ford who is still back by the bike. "OK, we've agreed to three stops at the different vendors. They're putting the cameras in the truck right now. You drive to three places around town. The painter, the chrome guy, and the upholsterer. Just drop off some bullshit parts, it's all fake, so don't worry about that. Chat the people up, flirt a little maybe, then come back. Ford and your crew will follow in the van. When you get to the shops, let the crew do everything first so they can get shots of you pulling in the parking lot, entering the building. Got it?"

"Yeah, sure. Are you coming with me?"

"Ah..." He hesitates. "No, Elise called, they need me up in Steamboat again, so I'm just gonna drive up there real fast and I'll be back soon. Tonight, probably, tomorrow at the latest."

"What? But it's far, right? You'll never be back that fast!"

"It's only three hours from here, Gidge. I swear, this is the last time, OK? She's just being a freak. I'll be right back. You'll be working anyway, you'll never miss me." And then he does it again. He leans down, kisses me on the cheek and walks off, calling out some last-minute bullshit to Spencer as he goes.

MANIC

I look back at Ford and he's frowning. He walks over to me. "I'll ride with you, Rook."

"No," I say. "I can drive myself, thanks."

The parts truck is a big-ass mother, red, with a huge ol' Shrike Bikes logo on it. It's like a twin to the one Spencer drives. It's even got flashy chrome exhaust pipes and rims. When I get in, I feel powerful.

I laugh. I have a thingy in my ear so I can hear Ford and a necklace with a microphone on it. They're worried about me getting lost even though they've punched all the addresses into the GPS, so he's talking in my ear as I get situated.

"What so funny?" he asks.

"I love this truck. I might have to buy me one. Ask Spencer if I can have it."

Ford repeats what I said and I can tell he's laughing. I barely make out Spencer's retort, but Ford repeats it for me. "He said if you help him get the full season, this will be one of the many signing bonuses he offers up for the contract."

I buckle myself in, then turn the ignition. The beast rumbles to life and I let out a little squeal. "OK, I'll do my best, Spence." Thankfully this thing is an automatic, so I put it in gear and gun it out of the parking lot, Ford and Spencer following along in the van with the crew, yelling in my ear to slow down.

But my foot has other ideas. I haven't driven in a while and I've never driven a truck. My lead foot is getting even heavier now, so the beast lurches forward with power. I roll my window down and pump my fist back at them as I whoop it up.

And promptly get flashing red and blue lights for my trouble.

"Oh, shit! The po-nine's here!"

"Rook," Ford says very seriously in my earpiece, "do you have a license?"

I pull off to the side of the totally abandoned road. How the hell did the cops even see me out here? We're like ten miles out of town. "Yes, but it's still Illinois."

The cop pulls in behind me and then the van pulls in behind the cop. Spencer jumps out and tries to run interference. He shakes hands with the cop and they walk up to my window together.

"Ma'am—" I'm suddenly having flashbacks of Ronin checking me for drugs and a laugh bursts out.

Spencer and the cop look at me funny.

"I'm not drinking, I swear."

"What?" the cop asks.

"I'm just saying, I'm not drunk or anything, officer. It's just I've never driven a truck like this before and it was so much fun, I got a little carried away." I stop to bat my eyelashes at him. "I'm sorry, I'll tone it down, OK?"

"License and registration."

Fucktard. I reach into my pocket and pull out my license and hand it over. Spencer's already on the other side of the truck fishing through the glove box for the insurance card and registration. When he finds them he hands the papers to me and I pass them along.

The cop takes them, eyeballing Spencer as he shuffles through the glove box, trying to hide a gun under some Dairy Queen napkins. "Please tell me that's not what I think it is."

"It's permitted, Scott. You wanna see my concealed carry card?"

"Only if it has *her* name on it, Spencer. She's the one driving the truck."

I glance over at Spencer and raise my eyebrows. He just shakes his head until the cop walks back to his car and gets inside.

"Goddamn it, Rook! You're on the road thirty seconds and you get pulled over!"

"Am I gonna get busted for that gun in the glove box?"

"I'm not sure. He could be a dick about that, but it's not technically illegal—we could fight it. I forgot it was in here to be honest, I have guns stashed everywhere. And you driving like Danica Patrick isn't fucking helping the situation. This might be

MANIC

the Wild West, but you can't piss off the locals like that, Rook!"

"That's not fair, Spencer! It's the middle of nowhere!" I look around trying to figure out where the cop came from but all I see is a little dirt road that leads up a hill and some cows munching on grass across the way.

"Well, if you'd listened to me when you were busy gunnin' it, I would've told you that a cop lives right up that road and that's where he eats his lunch every day."

"Oh."

Ford walks up and leans in my window. "This is good TV, Rook. Nice going."

"It wasn't a plan, you dickbitch," Spencer growls at him. "This guy hates my guts and he just saw my fucking piece in the glove box, so let's not piss him off, OK?"

We wait there in silence for what seems like eternity and then the cop finally comes back, writing something down on a pad of paper.

"Scott," Spencer says, trying to begin the negotiations that are surely coming. "Don't be an asshole. You know my trucks are legal, you know that gun is mine. She's new, she was having a little fun, she's—"

"She's got a missing person's report out on her in Illinois. Some guy who says he's her husband, Jon Walsh."

I lean out the window and puke right on Ford's shoes.

TWENTY-SIX

ROOK

"Rook?" Spencer and Ford are saying my name together but all I can do is try to remember how to breathe. "Rook? Stop, Rook. Look at me!"

"Get her out of the truck. Take her out!" The cop is pushing Ford to get out of the way and trying to open the door but I'm grasping onto the window and pulling in the opposite direction because I feel like I'm dying.

I'm dying.

He's found me.

I grab at Ford's shirt, pulling him towards me as I gasp for breath. "Help me! I can't—"

"She's just hyperventilating. Rook, look at me." I look up at the cop and he's pointing to his eyes. "Look at me, OK? Can you look at me?"

I nod, my breathing becoming harder and harder.

"Do you have any breathing conditions? Do I need to call an ambulance?"

MANIC

I shake my head as I continue to sob and gasp for air.

"OK. Listen, I'm not going to hurt you, I'm just going to put my hand over your mouth and pinch one nostril closed. Then you can only breathe through one side of your nose. This will help you calm down, OK?"

I nod and he does what he described. I struggle at first because it reminds me of being suffocated by Jon, but he keeps a firm hold over my mouth and talks to me in soft, soothing words. "Slow down, OK?" He looks me in the eyes. "Slow."

I try, but it's very hard to stop the chain reaction inside my body. I shake all over as I try my hardest to get my breathing under control. And then slowly, after many minutes, he removes his hand and I am not gasping.

And then I just cry. "He's gonna find me!"

I just cry.

"Rook," the cop says. "Don't cry, OK? No one's gonna find you. You're OK. If you start crying, you'll have another attack. Just calm down."

I stop the sobbing but the tears still come. They pour out in rivers and roll down my cheeks. "He's gonna find me. He's gonna know where I am!"

"Who, Rook?" Ford pushes the cop out of the way and puts his hand on my shoulder. "Who's gonna find you?"

"My ex, Jon. He's gonna know." I look over at the cop. "You ran my name and it triggered the report, right?"

"Yeah, but he won't have access to that, you don't—"

"He's a computer forensics specialist for the Chicago PD!"

The cop is stunned silent because I'm sure he's seen this scene play out a hundred times. There's only one reason for a girl to act this way about a man from her past.

"Scott, can we just take her home?" Spencer asks from the passenger seat. "If you're gonna write a ticket, do it fast, OK?"

"No, you're good." He looks past me, over to Spencer. "Sorry, dude. I had no idea. It was just a stupid traffic stop."

"Get in, Rook," Ford says, taking my arm. He opens the

door to the back cab and pushes me in, then follows me. "Drive, Spencer."

Spencer climbs over the console and plops down in the driver's seat and starts up the truck. He turns around and takes us back to the shop. When we get there, Ford talks into his little microphone and tells the crew to turn off the cameras. Then he and Spencer take me into the house and sit me down on the couch.

"OK, I'm not gonna fight with you about this, Rook," Ford says with a hard edge to his voice. "I'm only gonna ask you once. Is this man dangerous?"

I nod and the tears start again.

"How dangerous? Does he fight men? Or just women?"

"Just women, I think."

Both Ford and Spencer exchange a sort of conspiratorial look.

"Is he really your husband?"

I cry harder as I look up at Ford and nod. "He is. He made me!"

"OK, that's enough, Ford. She's had enough now. I'm calling Ronin. He's probably not even halfway yet." Spencer pulls out his phone and messes with the screen. We listen together as it dials Ronin on speaker.

It goes straight to voicemail.

"Shit, no service in the mountains. I'm not leaving this kind of message on voicemail, Rook. So we'll just have to wait until he gets back in range near Steamboat and I'll try again later."

I am suddenly exhausted and I just nod and lie down on the couch, my face buried in the pillow.

Ford sits down on the coffee table as Spencer goes outside to run interference with the camera crew coming up the front steps. "You're safe here, you know that right? You're totally safe here."

"I don't feel safe, Ford. I feel the opposite of safe."

"This is your damage, isn't it? You ran from *him*, didn't you?"

I nod my head into the pillow.

MANIC

"And somehow you found Ronin, and he figured it out. Because I know you didn't tell him. You're not a teller, are you, Rook? You keep secrets, don't you?"

"Just stop, Ford. I'm not in the mood."

He hesitates for a second, then takes a deep breath. "I have to confess, I've never seen someone have a panic attack like that. I thought you were dying."

I turn over a little so I can look up at his face. I'm not sure what I expect, but it isn't sympathy like I get. "I felt like I was dying, too. I thought you were a mental psychosis prodigy, Ford? How could you never've seen a panic attack?"

He laughs out a little bit of air. "I'm an armchair therapist—"

I watch him struggle for words for a few seconds and his eyes dart back and forth as he looks me in one eye, then the other. His expression becomes very serious. "What?" I ask.

"You really scared me."

"Sorry."

"You need to get a divorce."

"I can't see him again, Ford. I can't. I'm not just not capable of handling that. I'm not."

He looks away and looks off into the distance. "Just leave it to us, Rook. We'll handle it."

"What's that mean?"

Ford shrugs, like this is nothing. "I'm sure Ronin's going to ask for favors when he gets back."

"I don't understand."

"Just relax, OK? He won't hurt you again. You should just stop worrying about that right now."

"The hurt's inside, Ford. He doesn't need to be here to hurt me." I watch his expression carefully as he absorbs my words. This uncharacteristic version of Ford. The one who says he's scared and who talks soft and reassures me. I'm not sure who this guy is and it's making me nervous.

"Do you want me to leave you alone?"

I nod yes because my chest hurts with each hiccup of air left over from crying and hyperventilating and my eyes are burning so bad I can't keep them open anymore. "I just want to close my eyes, OK? Just for a minute."

"We'll be right outside if you need anything."

I turn away and face the back of the couch, running through all the bad days of my previous life. The psychological torture Jon put me through, the verbal lashings, the physical punishment. My head is throbbing so bad I almost want to throw up again.

But I think of Ronin instead. Of all the ways he's treated me nice since I met him. Even Ford, who is still a very weird guy who probably has some not-so-innocent intentions with me. But he's nice too, and he seems to care.

And Spencer, and Antoine, and Elise. Even Billy and Josie.

I have a whole new life filled with people are nice. People who don't think it's OK to hurt me.

But what if Jon decides he needs to hurt them too?

I start crying again, because I can handle him hurting me, but I would never be able to live with myself if he hurt one of my new friends.

TWENTY-SEVEN

RONIN

Clare's sleeping when I finally make it to the treatment center just past two. Antoine and Elise are already back at their little apartment and I'm not even gonna bother stopping in there, I just want to make sure Clare knows I'm still around. I sit down next her and smile when she begins to wake up. She's so much better than she was last week. Not out of the woods yet, but definitely better.

"You're back," she mumbles, still very drowsy from the methadone treatment.

"I said I would be. You didn't need to panic, you're gonna give Elise a heart attack, making her call me and threatening to stop treatment if I don't come."

"I was afraid you'd ditch me for that girl."

"Well, I wouldn't ditch you. It's not an either-or choice, Clare. You'll like her, you'll see."

"Are you staying?" She's having a hard time keeping her eyes open now, it's only a matter of time before she dozes off again.

MANIC

"No, sorry. I have to get back. But I'm rooting for you, you know that right?"

She's out. And it's a good thing, too. Because if she was at the tail end of her dose instead of at the onset, she'd be a lot harder to deal with. It sucks to say it, because it's all kinds of wrong, but she's so much nicer when she's sedated.

I go back out and tell the reception girl I'm leaving, then get back in my truck and start the three-hour drive all over again.

I've been trying not to think about Spencer's phone call, but it's hard not to, now that I'm heading back and there's nothing else to occupy my time. This makes the drive back to the Shrike Shop agonizing because all of the calm that came from seeing Clare asleep and getting better has been wiped away by Spencer's words. They just repeat over and over in my head. Panic attack. Missing person's report. Married.

That fucker *married* her.

The rage inside me as I picture her being legally tied to that violence is almost too much and by the time I pull the truck into the driveway, I'm ready to kick someone's ass.

Ford and Spence break from the crowd of crew members out near the shop and start walking towards me. I just stand still, trying to calm myself. Spencer recognizes the look on my face and jerks his head out towards the woods.

It's like *deja vu* as the three of us veer off the driveway and head north towards the little bend in the river. Even when we meet up, we say nothing, just continue walking until we are under the cover of the trees. Once there we follow the little footpath down to the river bank— the sound of rushing water just loud enough to layer over our words and make them unintelligible should anyone be listening.

Old habits.

I look at Ford, then Spence, and state matter-of-factly in a low voice, "This dude's gettin' wiped. Let's vote."

"I'm in," Spence says.

"I'm in," Ford says.

"I'll wait and talk to her, of course, but I don't see a way around it. It's done."

We walk back out, part ways in the middle of the yard, and I head to the house and they veer off back to the party.

I stand outside for a minute to calm myself, then reach down and pick a pink daisy from the front garden. It's just a weedy little thing, half wilted from the afternoon sun, but I want to brighten up her day and this is all I have.

I open the door quietly. Spence said she was asleep on the couch the last time I talked to him on the phone, so I make my way over to the living room and ease myself down in the large leather chair across the room.

When she told me what happened to her back in Chicago I processed it, then tucked it away. I've met lots of asshole guys who hit girls. I've met lots of girls who get hit. But I've only ever dated one besides Rook.

That's how I caught on to her erratic behavior so fast when she showed up. I knew the first moment I saw her crouching down in that stairwell outside the studio door that someone had mistreated her. But I had no idea how sick that fucker really was until she told me about the beating that finally convinced her to leave.

She made it clear that she wasn't interested in getting the guy back or putting him away. And I don't blame her one bit. But I should never have agreed to her request. And I have no excuse. Spencer was right there. Ford was on his way. It was almost too perfect.

But maybe a blessing in disguise. We know what we're up against now. Computer forensics specialist with the Chicago PD is nothing to dismiss and had we not know that little detail before making plans, we'd almost certainly be fucked.

But we are far from fucked now.

Rook inhales quickly several times, proof of her earlier panic attack betraying her resting body.

I'm shaking, that's how pissed off I am. I want to kill someone.

MANIC

I rub my hands across my face and take out my phone to text the accountant. I instruct him to move all her money to her bank account, put it all in plain sight—to hell with the penalties, just move that shit now. I'll pay her back.

The secret to the perfect job is to keep it easy. Very predictable.

I've thought about this job all the way down the mountain. And I might not know him all that well, but if he's a hacker he's into two things. The thrill of penetrating security firewalls and money.

Rook's got a nice little stash of money right now. Only fifty grand or so, but still. If you could steal fifty grand in an afternoon and be guaranteed to get away with it, you would.

And he will.

Men who hit women are also easy to read, I know this from the very first job Spence, Ford and I pulled just before Mardee died. Those assholes think their women are property. This Jon guy sees Rook as something he owns.

In my opinion this is the perfect combination. Half money-lusting hacker, half misogynist woman-beater.

Because that makes him vulnerable to money and sex.

Two things I can most definitely dangle in front of him, then twist it around so bad, he'll never know what hit him.

This is what we used to do.

Your first impression of Spencer should be dumb. There's just no way around that, in high school he always looked the part of the big dumb jock. And now that he's all tatted up, he's just switched over to being the big dumb biker.

Your first impression of Ford should be well-dressed asshole, but maybe a little on the weak side. Not buff like Spence, but lean and fast. He plays that part well. Snooty, rich, privileged, soft hands, soft words, living off his name and his family's wealth.

Your first impression of me should be honest, trustworthy guy. Good-looking, charming, happy, and eager to help and please. A rule-follower who wants to forget where he came from.

Your first impressions would be dead-ass wrong in all three

cases.

Because Spencer is a certifiable genius, Ford is as ruthless as they come, and I'm an accomplished liar.

Together we pulled off a series of con jobs in college that netted us tens of millions of dollars—in secret, untraceable bank accounts, of course.

And I have a plan for this Jon guy.

Oh, yes, I think to myself as I twirl the pink daisy by its stem between my fingers.

I most certainly do have a motherfucking plan for this guy.

TWENTY-EIGHT

ROOK

I wake suddenly, the rush of my earlier panic attack making me sit straight up before I realize where I am. The dying sunlight from outside filters through the sheer curtains but it's dusky inside as well. Ronin is sitting across the living room from me. I smile at him, trying my hardest not to cry as the words come out. "You came."

He gets up and walks over to the couch, then sits down and sets my head in his lap. "Of course I came, Gidget. I'm so sorry I wasn't there for you." He drags a piece of hair off my forehead and then tucks it behind my ear with a little pink daisy.

My hand goes to the flower and I am overwhelmed with how much he means to me. "I'm sorry," I choke out between half-hidden sobs.

He lets out a soft chuckle and leans down to kiss my forehead. "What in the world do you have to be sorry for?"

"For not telling you I was legally married."

He sighs. "I won't pretend, it hurt a little to find that out from

MANIC

Spencer over the phone, but Rook, we barely know each other. It's not like you lied, it just never came up."

"So you're not mad at me?"

"No, Gidge. I'm not mad. We can talk about that stuff later. How are you feeling?"

I swallow down all my feelings and paint on a happy face. "I'm OK." He's staring down at me with a scowl. "What?"

"You don't look OK, Rook. Tell me the truth now."

The tears build up again and my whole face scrunches up as I try to stop them. "I'm scared, Ronin." He strokes my hair and waits for me to continue, so I take a deep breath. "Why can't he just go away? Why? How arrogant can he be? To put out a missing person's report on me after what he did? It's like he's still claiming me, you know?"

"He's not getting you. Ever. He's never coming near you again, Rook, so just put that thought out of your mind, OK?"

"But now he knows I'm here. There's a missing person's report, what does that mean? Will I have to go back?"

"No, Rook. The report has been cleared now, he knows it was cleared here in Larimer County, and that's it. Spencer and Ford already talked to the deputy who pulled you over and he said they have to file a report because they cleared the missing persons out of the database, but that's all they're required to do. They won't mention Spencer or the shop or anything."

I breathe out a little sigh of relief, but Ronin's not done talking yet. "But the problem is, you told everyone he's a computer forensics specialist?"

I nod up at him as my stomach roils with this 'but'.

"He *has* to know where you are. There's no way he doesn't know where you are. You've done nothing to hide yourself, your social's on record as working for us, you have a bank account…"

My whole face crumples under this news. "Oh, God."

"But look at it this way, Rook. He hasn't bothered you so he's probably given up."

I snort through my sobs. "He didn't give up. You don't

understand. He threatened me! He tried to—"

I stop, because even though this is Ronin and I know he's one hundred percent on my side, admitting that I allowed this monster to do these things to me is so hard. It makes me feel so weak and stupid.

Ronin strokes my cheek. "He tried to what?" he asks softly. "Just tell me, Rook. I'm not gonna judge you and I know it must be hard to talk about, but we need to know what we're up against."

"I didn't want to marry him." I look up at Ronin, pleading with him to believe me. "I didn't. But he took me up to this island in the lake near Michigan, some stupid island where they have no cars. And he told me it was for my birthday, when I turned eighteen. Before that we sorta had to hide because he was already twenty-one when we started dating." I stop and meet Ronin's worried eyes. "I was only sixteen. But I was in a bad foster home and I ran away. I'm not even sure how it happened, but next minute I was on the streets homeless, just wandering around. And I begged enough money to go inside this diner and get some food, and he was sitting next to me at the counter. I knew it was stupid then, but I was desperate. So I let him take me home.

"It was OK for a while. I turned seventeen a few months later, and he moved us to that dumpy house his uncle left him when he died. And then all the violence and weird shit started. He was always talking about marriage and at first I said no, I'm too young. But after a while that got me a smack and a long lecture about how I belonged to him. So I just agreed. Then he booked this trip to that island for my eighteenth birthday and when we got there we were staying in the honeymoon cabin at this crappy campground on the lake. And—"

I shake my head as I remember it.

"Tell me, Rook."

I look up at Ronin and just blurt it out. "He tried to drown me. He held me under the water that night, he choked me. I thought I was gonna die, Ronin. I swear. He said he'd kill me if I didn't agree to marry him and if I ever tried to leave him, he'd

MANIC

torture me. And I believed him because he had already done so many terrible, *terrible* things to my body by that time, drowning and torture were just the next logical steps."

Ronin brings his hands up and scrubs them across his face a few times but he says nothing.

"Please, Ronin, tell me what you're thinking right now. Do you hate me?"

He leans down and kisses my forehead one more time. "No, Rook. Hating you is the last thing I'm thinking about. I'm thinking about how easy it would be for us to kill that motherfucker."

"Us? As in me and you?"

He's got a far-off gaze now, just staring out into space. "No, Gidge. Us, as in Spencer, Ford, and me." He looks down and his eyes are blazing with anger. "It would be so easy, you have no idea."

I think back to what Ford said earlier. *I'm sure Ronin's going to ask for favors when he comes back.* "What do you mean by that, Ronin?"

He sighs and ignores my question. "You wanna stay here tonight? Or you wanna go home? It's only an hour and a half drive home. Wanna go home?"

"What about the footage we need for the show?"

"Fuck the show. We can do that another day."

"But we have to do it though, right? So let's just stay here and do that tomorrow and then it can be over with."

He gets up and takes my hand, pulling me up with him. "Come on, then. Let's wash your face and get something to eat. You hungry?"

I nod and let him take care of everything. There's nothing about this night I want to be responsible for, I just want him to do all of it.

After I splash some cold water on my face and wash off the dirt and tears, Ronin leads me out to the fire pit near the shop where the crews have a big BBQ going. Everyone is standing around joking and drinking. Even Spencer and Ford have eased in with the crowd. No one seems to know that I had a major meltdown or that my ex is a piece of shit woman-beater and is looking for me so he can come back and finish the job. So I just pack all that bad stuff away and quietly stick to Ronin's side.

It feels normal.

Ronin does this.

Ronin makes me feel normal.

TWENTY-NINE

RONIN

We finish filming late the next day and then we all pile into our vehicles and go back home. Spencer stays one more night since the frame came in from painting and he wanted to start the assembly, but he's back on duty with us bright and early this morning.

Ford has given in to Rook completely. She gets to stay with me. No cameras in the apartment.

Ford is weirdly affected by all this Rook stuff. It hits us all pretty close to home, watching her fall to pieces. It brings back a lot of very bad memories of Mardee and how all that shit went down in the end.

How Ford lost and I won.

But really, no one won. We all lost.

I got Mardee, I took her from Ford, and I lost her anyway.

Rook was wrong the other day when she asked what Ford did to start our fight. It wasn't Ford who did anything. It was me. I'm the one who took Mardee from him, brought her into

MANIC

the studio, then let her get caught up in the life, the money, the drugs, and the sex—only to discard her and leave her to find her own way back from all the scumbags that hover around the periphery of the modeling and entertainment worlds.

He never forgave me, and up until right now—maybe even right this second as I run all this through my head again—I never gave a fuck. I could always take or leave Ford, he was barely an acquaintance and never a friend.

But despite that he was a partner in the business the three of us ran during college.

That was just before Mardee died. Just the one job, we said, just the one guy, the dealer who turned Mardee on to the heroin. We were all feeling guilty. Spence for bringing her around the guys in this neighborhood, Ford for letting me take her away, and me for not caring enough about her to stop what was happening right in front of my face.

But we were all a little lost after Mardee died, and that job was too easy, because regardless of what Spencer looks like on the outside, the fact is, he's a fucking certifiable genius on the inside.

Ford might just be a well-dressed asshole to most people, but if you saw the guy's psychological profile, you'd shit your pants. I've seen it—that's how I know he's one fucked-up individual. He showed it to me, walked me right into his old man's office, hacked into his computer, and let me read what his own father wrote about him.

Incapable of emotion—high-functioning Asperger's Syndrome with areas of prodigious savant skills.

Like Spencer, Ford is a genius, but unlike Spencer, Ford's brand of intelligence is scary high. Off-the-charts evil-genius kinda shit. The kind of intelligence that comes about once every few hundred years.

But even though Ford has some emotional limitations, he's perceptive to fitting in. He started failing his intelligence tests long before I ever met him. In fact, that file in his father's computer was created when he was only seven years old. Ford never passed another test after that. He hides both his limitations and abilities well.

Showing me that personal file was his way of making things right for that fucked-up prank he pulled on me in high school. But we can all thank his solitary childhood computer geek stage for the special skills he brings to the table now.

Me? I'm not a genius, I'm not a hacker, I'm just the face. But every operation needs a front man, right?

And this Jon Walsh asshole is a worthy opponent. It might even be fun.

I watch Rook and Ford cross the street and then part ways at Ford's little sports car. Rook looks up, sees me watching, then drops her head. I'm not jealous of Ford. If she wants to work out with him, that's her deal. I won't interfere. But that doesn't mean I won't keep my eye on her as she does it.

I stay on the terrace until I hear the door in the apartment beep, then go inside and meet her in the shower.

"Have a nice run?"

"Yes," she says as she takes her clothes off and then gets in. It's just a regular single stream of water, so I take it she doesn't want company and go get dressed. Today is the cyborg bike shoot. It's an amazing custom chopper that's been in the inventory the longest since it was Spencer's first custom bike, and I know he's really counting on this photo to sell the thing soon. So Rook and I will have to be on today.

Trouble is, she's not on at all. She's so off, it's getting dark in there quick. She said almost nothing on the way home yesterday, and it wasn't because of the cameras, because Ford took them out of the truck before we left.

When we went to bed last night I wasn't expecting sex, not after her fucked-up weekend. But I wasn't expecting the cold shoulder either. I had to tug her up next to me. She settled after that, but up until last night, I've never had to encourage it. I don't even want to think about what that might mean.

MANIC

I wait patiently in the living room as she exits the shower and dresses in some shorts and a tank top. She doesn't even bother with shoes, just grabs my hand when she gets to the door and we walk downstairs together. "You OK?" I ask as we cross the empty studio.

"Yeah, I think so."

I squeeze her hand. "It's a long day. You're a cyborg today."

She smiles but says nothing.

Spencer is messing with the tunes when we walk in and all the crews are busy checking sound and lighting and all that other bullshit they do for the TV show filming. I take a seat on the couch I had a crew member move in over the weekend. I figured if Ford and I had to sit around and watch, we might as well be comfortable. He's not around when we come in, probably still down the street at his corporate apartment.

"What do ya want to listen to today, Rook?" Spencer calls out to her as she goes into the half-hearted attempt at a dressing room and changes into the little robe.

"I don't care. Whatever you want, Spence."

Spencer looks at me after she turns away from him. I shrug.

"Well, that's not an answer, Blackbird. I need an answer. Choose a band."

She turns back, clearly confused at his insistence. "Um." She stops to think. "Lady Gaga?"

I hold down a snort.

"What?" she asks me, annoyed. "I like her."

I throw up my hands in an *I surrender* gesture, then kick my feet up on the coffee table as Ford walks in.

"Did you just say Lady Gaga, Rook? I love her."

I turn and sneer at him. What a dick.

"But I have a better idea."

"What?" Rook asks, a little defeated by my reaction to her choice in music. I'm the dick and now I feel like shit.

"I'll read to you."

Rook immediately smiles and I'm like, *What the fuck? Read*

to her gets a smile, but me wanting to take a shower gets a big fat nothing?

"It's a joke, Ronin. Relax," Spence says. "Rook was making fun of his reading list last week."

"Yeah," she says. "You were gone that day. With Clare."

Ouch.

She takes her attention back to Ford. "Is it a billionaire book?" She smirks at him.

Smirks.

And everyone laughs but me. Not in on the joke again.

"No," Ford says through his smile. "It's *Gatsby*. You interested? You never read it, you said."

She sighs and shrugs. "I'd rather you read that one about Rowdy the hot spelunker, but whatever."

Ford is either an evil genius for reminding Rook that I left her last week, or a clueless dumb fuck.

I think we've already established which of those he is.

"OK," he says, taking a seat next to me. "Oh." He looks over my way this time. "I've catered lunch. Rook looks thin, she's not eating enough."

I look over at Spencer and he's shaking his head at me. "Don't do it, Ronin. He's baiting you."

I look over at Rook and she's waiting to see how I'll handle this little remark. What can I say? "Awesome, looking forward to Ford footing the bill for lunch."

Maybe I should go running with them in the morning, because clearly they had quite the conversation while I was back at the studio. And yeah, he's right. She looks a little thinner, but he's implying I'm not keeping track of her. He's implying I'm too busy with Clare to notice.

And he'd be right. Because I haven't weighed her in weeks.

Ford starts reading, Spencer grabs his paints and brushes, and Rook disrobes.

Our day begins.

Ford is adept at narrating books. He really missed his calling

MANIC

in voiceovers. He brings the book to life as Rook listens, cocking her head at all the right moments, internally questioning all the carefully planned foreshadowing, and even stopping him on two occasions to ask a question.

Fucking Ford.

He finishes the book long before Spencer is done painting up Rook's cyborg body and this is the perfect time for everyone to take a break. Spencer offers to walk Rook over to the bathrooms down the hall so I take my attention to Ford as he messes with that stupid e-reader.

"What?" he asks, without looking up at me.

"What are you doing, Ford? You trying to steal her right out from under me, or what? I mean, come on—Mardee was a long time ago..."

He looks up at her name. "Don't," he says, shaking his head. "Don't you fucking dare accuse me of that shit. I'm worried about Rook—"

"You're forgetting something, Ford. You're incapable of being worried about anyone, so save your bullshit for the person who doesn't understand you're an emotionless freak."

"I've invested a lot of time and money, not to mention my reputation with this show, in *her*. Maybe you don't care about this project, but Spencer and I do. So I'm not going stand by and watch her fall apart because you were too busy with that pathetic drug-addicted princess of yours to give a fuck."

I stand up and Ford follows.

"You want to fight, Ronin?" He stares me in the face. "I'm the guy you *need*, remember? I'm the only guy who matters in all this. So sit your ass down and shut the fuck up."

My head is throbbing, that's how pissed off I am. The blood is rushing to my head and I feel like I'm gonna explode if I don't just put my fist through his teeth. I poke him in the chest, a provocation, but Ford has a lot more self-discipline than I ever did. He can't be baited. "You better make it happen then, because I'll tell you what, if I have to put up with you pulling this stealthy girlfriend-stealing bullshit all summer, then you better come through."

He smiles. "If she *can* be stolen, then she was never yours to begin with. And do not insult my skills or question my ability to *come through*. I always come through."

Rook and Spencer come back in, chatting about the bike. I guess they went upstairs to see it real fast. Or maybe Spencer knew Ford and I were gonna get into it and he took her far enough away so she didn't have to see it.

"What now, Rook?" Spence asks. "Story or music?"

"What else you have on that thing, Ford?" She wanders over and sits down next to me. I put my hand on her shoulder and rub her back a little. She shudders and then leans into my chest.

"Watch the paint, Rook!" Spencer calls.

She sits up and looks back at me apologetically. "You're bored, huh?"

"Not at all, Gidget. Not at all." I smile at her. She's totally naked, but she's covered in so much paint right now, it's easy to forget. "Pick—story or music."

"Story," she says, glancing back at Ford. "Rowdy the Spelunker and that virgin chick."

"Ashley," Ford chimes in.

Rook laughs. "You've been reading it!"

He shakes his head and she giggles at him. Giggles.

"How about *The Secret Garden?*" he asks in a low voice.

Now she loses it, her laugh is so big even I have to smile. I look over at Ford and he knows he just won. He knows it.

"You'll read *The Secret Garden* to me?" She squints her eyes at him in disbelief.

"Yes, go, let Spencer finish so we can be done."

And Ford does read that stupid girly childhood book to her. Every motherfucking flowery word of it. And this time Rook's face is more than interested and questioning.

She's enchanted.

THIRTY

ROOK

Spencer has painted me up as a cyborg.

It's one hundred percent awesome. As in, I might die from feeling so cool right now. He's such a master with that paintbrush, he knows just where to put the colors to make his art look 3D. He paints tubes and stuff all down my midsection, then fills in behind that with shades of black and blue, so it looks like I'm hollow. Like my midsection is nothing but these tubes and wires. He does the same thing to my arms, making them look like pistons and mechanical parts in some place, devoid of skin. Then purely human in others.

When he takes me up to see the bike after our bathroom break it's a cyborg too, only the opposite of me. I'm mostly girl with machine parts, but the bike is mostly bike with girl parts. In fact, this bike is a girl. Well, a girl of the cyborg persuasion. She's bent over at the hips and her arms reach down, acting as the front fork that holds the tire. He head acts as the headlight, and her back is the tank, but it looks a lot like my stomach at the

MANIC

moment. Parts of it are painted in just the right way to make it look like it's got a huge hole in it, with tubes and piston visible.

I actually clap at this one and make a remark to Spencer that it's very *Terminator 2*.

He loves that and has to stifle a proud grin with his fist.

Today I'm really happy to be a part of this project. Spencer is amazing. The Shrike bikes are stunning. And his artwork is incredible. I hope Antoine gives me some of these photos, because this is something I'd like to remember forever.

Maybe the bikinis were pretty boring and exploitative, but this is definitely more like movie FX.

And then there's Ford.

This morning at the stadium we talked a lot. Much more than usual. Not about me, not at all. But about him. I asked him about his schooling and he told me all about CU Boulder and their film department. He even went so far as to say he could get me in to talk to someone.

He even hinted at an internship next summer.

How incredible would that be?

I jerk back to reality as Spencer asks me to tilt my head up so he can paint my face. Ford is still reading.

And I tell you what, this whole *let me read to you* thing is just about the most tender expression I've ever experienced with a man. I'm not sure why, maybe because of the book. It's such a sweet book, so opposite of Ford in every way, that the fact that he's willing to read those words out loud, just to make me happy, well—it does something to me.

It doesn't want to make me jump his bones, but it does add to the ever-growing, and ever-changing, view I have of Ford.

Ronin is not happy. But I don't care. I don't want Ford. I'm not in love with him, I'm not even fantasizing about kissing him or touching him or anything like that. I'm just not interested in him that way. I'm interested in Ronin that way. So I don't feel bad about these new feelings for Ford. Ronin will have to get over it because Ford and I might become friends.

"OK, Blackbird. You're ready for your close-up."

I smile at the movie reference. I look over at Ronin and he's asleep.

"Should we let him get his beauty rest?" Ford asks. "I can walk you upstairs and fill in for Ronin in the shoot. You haven't posed with me yet."

"Um, that's a big negative, Ford. Ronin?" I shake him a little.

"I'm awake!" he says, sitting up.

"Right," I laugh. "We're ready to go upstairs." Ford heads out ahead of us and Ronin gets up and takes my hand, still not fully awake. "You're tired from all that driving, huh?"

He smiles. "It's catching up with me. But we're in the home stretch now, Gidge. We'll crash soon."

"I'm pretty tired too, that was the longest painting session yet. Do you have to get ready?"

"Just your basic futuristic road warrior shit, nothing like you, my cyborg sex kitten."

"I love this one. I feel like…"

"A cyborg sex kitten?"

"Yeah," I say, snickering. I really am a cyborg sex kitten because my girls are painted up with huge blue nipples and the clothing Spencer painted on is more like small strips of metallic blue fabric that criss-cross my body in all the wrong places. Which means, to the men, all the right places. None of the fun bits are covered by the fake fabric in the least. My legs are painted up to look like I'm wearing ripped blue leggings, and I have painted boots that come up just past my ankle. "I don't really *look* like her, but I *feel* like a cyborg Tank Girl."

"Mmmm, I crushed on her pretty hard back in the day. She's hot."

We part ways in the studio, I go to Josie for hair—no makeup because Spencer painted my face this time—and Ronin goes to the dressing room to change. We meet in front of the bike about thirty minutes later and Ronin is absolutely the sexiest Terminator that ever existed. "I need your clothes, your boots,

MANIC

and your motorcycle," I quote from the movie, snickering under my breath.

"What'd you say, Gidget?"

"Oh." I blush. "Did I say that out loud?"

He grins down at me and takes my hand. "Let's make this fun, wanna make it fun?"

"I could use some fun, actually."

He leans into me and begins to kiss my neck, his hands lightly exploring my body, just barely skimming my skin so he doesn't disturb the paint. I arch my back and tip my head and his hand slides up and caresses my throat.

"Sorry," he says as he moves his hand away.

I'm just about to ask what he meant by that when Antoine starts giving us directions in French and there's no time, because I lose track of everything but Ronin's words. They are soft and slow, not anything like our last shoot when it was his hands that got me excited. He's tender with cyborg sex-kitten Rook. I slide against him and he strokes my cheek with the side of his index finger and then he leans in and kisses me.

It's not bruising or deep, but just a flicker, his tongue darting forward just enough to tease me, twisting against my lips, then pulling back so I'm left wanting more. He strokes my hair as he watches me with a question in his eyes.

"What's wrong?" I ask.

He shakes his head and scoots my whole body forward so my pelvis is pressing right up against him. But it's what I don't feel that surprises me. He's not excited. "What's wrong, Ronin?"

"Nothing's wrong." He takes his nibbles down my neck and then over to my ear, breathing a soft breath against the tender skin, and sends a chill through my whole body. His hands circle my waist and then he whispers, "Lean back, Gidge."

I do as he asks. His strong hands keep my lower body firm against his groin while my upper body lowers down onto the tank. I'm an arch, the blue nipples pointing straight up. Then Ronin's mouth is all over my stomach, licking and nipping the skin on my belly, teasing me and sending little chilly flutters shooting up my arms.

One hand moves away from my waist and he slides one finger up my ribcage, tracing the bones one at a time in such a way that I actually squirm away and giggle at the tickle. The other hand moves away from my waist now too, only this one slides up my stomach and grabs my breast just as the weight of his body lowers down on me.

Every time we shoot these erotic scenes together he surprises me because it's never, ever the same scenario twice.

And while the heady, lustful passionate shoots are fun and say *I want to jump your bones right now*, this one is soft and sexy in a very tender way that says *I want you to be part of my life forever*.

THIRTY-ONE

RONIN

I'm not sure what possesses me to palm her throat like that in the shoot, but as soon as I do it, I'm ashamed. And then the last time we made love hits me hard. When I blindfolded her and wanted to assert more control.

She tried to tell me she wasn't into that crap but I pushed.

And now I'm so fucking ashamed.

I've been thinking about her relationship with that Jon fucker since she told me he tried to drown her and it's taken a lot of self-control to keep it tucked away. As soon as Antoine dismisses us I take her hand and lead her upstairs to my apartment and walk her over to the shower.

"God, it's such a shame to wash this all off right now, don't you think, Ronin?"

She's worried about Spencer's artwork. It kills me how this girl forces herself to cope. "Yeah, but that's why we take the pictures. Spencer will always have the pictures."

She looks at me funny. "What's the matter with you?"

MANIC

"Nothing, why?"

"You're being weird."

I turn on the shower and start stripping. "What makes you say that?"

She looks down as I take off my pants. "Well, you're not excited to see me." She laughs a little at this. "And nothing we were doing out there was turning you on. Are you mad at me?"

I kick off my boxers and lean down to kiss her. "Absolutely not, I'm not mad. I'm just sorry about that choke move out there. And the whole blindfold and spanking thing we did last time. I'm not sure why you put up with me."

"Wait, what'd I miss? What choke move? And I sorta liked that spanking stuff."

I guide her into the shower and start washing off her paint. It's thick this time, her whole body is covered. I start with her back. "I'm just not comfortable with it, Gidge. Not after what he did to you for all those years."

"What're you talking about?"

"The rape. I'm surprised you can even tolerate me kissing you, let alone that dominant bullshit I tried to pull."

"Ronin, he didn't really rape me."

"No? So you gave him permission to have sex with you after all that violence?"

"Well, no, but I was his wife. And before that, I never told him no."

"Because you wanted to have sex with him?"

"No! Of course not. Even before he got violent I never wanted to sleep with him. I was a virgin."

I turn away to hide my anger but the words still come out. "He took your virginity by rape?"

"He didn't rape me, Ronin. I never told him no."

"Did you tell him yes?"

"Well no, but—"

"Rook, he *raped* you. Repeatedly, for several years. You're just so used to being mistreated you can't even comprehend what happened."

She stares at me, the water running down her face, streaking it with black and blue paint that slides down her body and swirls together in an inky pool of color at her feet.

"He raped you."

She shakes her head. "No."

I reach out and pull her close, hug her tightly. "Yes. That's what happened, Rook. And while I'm very proud of you for how well you've been dealing with the past, you need to know, in case it ever happens again, that if a man intimidates you into sex, that. Is. Rape."

She pulls back, squinting her eyes up at me as she tries to process my words. "I don't think I can talk about this."

I nod and pick up the sponge, then swipe it down her arm. She stands still as I wash her. Just thinking about what I said.

We meet Spencer and Ford for dinner, and even though they both keep up their ends of the conversation with some crude *South Park* talk, Rook is unable to hide her reaction to the facts that are suddenly becoming clear.

The doctors say the brain finds way to cope with stress and one of those ways, a very popular way actually, is denial.

This girl has been in denial for so long, she can barely process the truth.

When we go to bed that night she's quiet and clingy. I like her clingy because that just means I get to touch her more. But she's not snuggling, she's desperately holding on to me. She sighs against my chest and I sigh with her.

It hurts me—physically hurts me—to think of what she went through as a teenager.

She was a child when that monster found her, desperate and needy. Homeless and hungry, alone on the streets.

MANIC

And that pathetic excuse of a human is nothing more than a pedophile rapist.

It takes hours for Rook to slide into her normal deep sleep, but I wait patiently until her breathing evens out, her clenched fist releases my shirt, and she turns a little to sink into the pillow. I slip out of bed, grab my phone and text Ford.

He's standing down in the studio near the far windows, like he never went home. He knows better than to speak about work unless the conditions are right, so he walks to the center of the room and flips on one of the fans we use for windy shoots.

"What'd ya got?" I ask, my voice barely audible over the vibrating hum.

"A nibble. Small withdrawal."

"He's testing?"

"Yes, that's my guess."

"So did you make a grab?"

He sneers at me. "If we just established he's testing, why the fuck would I grab him now?"

"I'm just asking, Ford."

"Be patient. It's a waiting game. He knows where she is now, the ball's in our court. I'll put the website up this week and set up the accounts. See if we can't tempt him to move fast."

"Do you think he will?'

Ford looks out the window as he thinks. "No, I think he's gonna wait. I think he's one paranoid motherfucker, but stratospherically ballsy at the same time."

"Why?"

"Because his first transaction was ninety-nine cents. He went inside and paid for a cup of coffee at Cookie's with a card from Rook's account with his name on it. I found it on the security footage we have access to for the show. I don't want to risk invading Rook's account because I'll muddy the tracks, so I can't be sure of how he got it without asking Rook to check things, but there's only one reason for him to be that ballsy. And that's because he ordered that extra card right from her online banking account. He's definitely had access to that for a while now."

"What a dumbass."

"Yeah, that's what *we* think because we know the food's free at Cookie's, so she'd never pay for a cup of coffee. It was a dead giveaway, we couldn't have asked for a better tip-off. But in his mind, that's about the safest transaction there is. A cup of coffee at her local haunt. If she did pay for food there, she'd never suspect it."

"How long do you think? Before he moves on her?"

"Hard to tell." Ford shrugs. "But he's quite good, it takes some skill to deal directly with banks."

"What about the other stuff?"

Ford smiles his nasty evil genius smile and nods his head. "Setting it up. He'll regret ever stepping into my little sphere of vengeance."

I get the shivers as the words come out because Ford is diabolical when it comes to these jobs. "What do you want me to do?"

"This is a non-personal con, Ronin. You're not really necessary until the very end. Just keep your eyes open, I don't trust this man. He's devious. And we all need to be carrying from now on. He was issued a concealed carry weapons permit out of the JeffCo Sheriff last week."

"Fuck. That means he's been here for a while."

"Probably as long as Rook has. That's the only way he could get that permit so quickly, and even then, he probably had someone pull strings."

I just nod, hoping we're not putting her in more danger as this plays out.

Ford turns and walks off and I flick the fan off and take the stairs three at a time back up to my apartment.

Rook is still sleeping peacefully, unaware of the deal Ford, Spence, and I are making. Unaware of who I really am, what I used to do, and what I'm capable of.

Unaware of what I'm gonna do for her now.

THIRTY_TWO

RONIN

And that's pretty much how our summer passes. We put the entire studio on lockdown, no public hours at all anymore, entrance by appointment only. Spence, Ford and I hold secret meetings under cover of bubbling rivers or oscillating fans. Rook is painted up to match the bike of the day and then photographed alone or sitting in my lap. We spend our weekends up at the Shrike Shop, filming fake deliveries and goofing off for the cameras. I visit Clare up in Steamboat a few times as a reward for good behavior. She finally begins to make progress towards a real recovery.

And we wait it out.

We wait for that sick fuck to make his move.

But he is so very, very patient.

And it's making me very nervous, because there's no way around it. Somehow, some way, this asshole knows we're setting him up. Ford was supposed to move on to part two of the con more than a month ago, but Jon Walsh disappeared and we had

MANIC

to hold back, then start all over again when he finally resurfaced. Ford says it's normal for a guy with his credentials to be wary, but I'm not buying it. There's no way this is normal.

So I worry, and pace, and most nights I sit up in bed, watching Rook sleep, my Ruger in hand. Like I am right fucking now. Maybe this started out with him paranoid, but I have a bad feeling that he's turned the tables on us, like somehow he knows. He knows who we are and what we do and he's taunting us.

And our road trip to Sturgis starts today, so that means we're gonna be out of state, on the highway, in a campground with five thousand other strangers—all badass, all mean as fuck, all drunk and horny—and this is not going to end well. I can feel it.

I drag my hand across my forehead to wipe the sweat and Rook breathes a little heavier than normal, like she's dreaming. She's a perceptive girl, that's one thing I noticed about her immediately. She reads body language like a librarian reads books. She's on to us.

But anytime she asks, we shut her down. And something tells me she's OK with that. She's at the very end of her coping capabilities, she wants us to handle it for her.

She still runs with Ford in the mornings, but now Spencer and I hang out over there too, just in case. The AM training program at Coors Field is not something most people know about. It's private, reserved for big shots in the know. But this Jon guy seems to be in the know more often than not.

The waiting is killing me.

My phone buzzes with a text and my heart jumps at the noise.

Fucking Ford. I read the text and it simply says: *Nibble, nibble.*

He's such a child. I text back: *Don't fuck it up this time.*

I didn't fuck it up last time, asshole. Part two, commencing now. Website accessed.

I click the link Ford sends and almost get physically ill when I see Rook's picture advertising a live sex cam. I grimace and look over at her again. If she knew, she'd probably hate me. I close the web browser down and sneak out of bed. Light is already filtering through the windows and since we're leaving for Sturgis later this morning, I might as well just get up and go find Ford and talk this shit out with him in person.

"Rook," I whisper down in her ear. "Wake up, Gidge."

"Hmmm."

"I'm going down the studio for a second, but the alarm is still set, so if I'm not back, don't ignore it. We gotta get ready to go in about an hour. OK?"

Nothing but snores.

"Rook!"

"Mmm-hmmm. Heard you."

"And do not ignore me if I text."

More snores.

"Fuck it, I'll be right back, OK?"

She's out.

I slip some jeans on and walk out to the hallway and make my way down to the garden terrace, texting Ford as I go. When I get outside he's over on the far side, craning his neck to see something down the street. The edginess is back and my heart beats a little faster. "What's up?" I ask softly as I near him.

"Saw someone. Maybe him, actually." He takes his attention to a ping on his tablet, scans the message, then turns back to the street below.

My heart rate jacks up as I process his words. "You're fucking kidding me? Now?"

"I said *I think*, Ronin."

"Where's Spence?"

"I sent him down the street, that's who I was watching."

"Did Walsh make a purchase?"

"Not yet, but I've had seventeen nibbles on it in the past several hours."

"Define nibble, Ford. What's that even mean?"

Ford stops his intense concentration on the street and turns to me. "He's tried to hack it repeatedly over night. But my friend

MANIC

is mistaken if he thinks he can crack past my firewall machine before I'm ready to let him in."

"So he wants cam access but doesn't want to pay and leave a record."

"Pretty much," Ford says, turning back to the street. Spencer is in plain sight now, walking back towards us.

"Well, that pretty much defeats the whole fucking purpose of having that site in the first place, doesn't it? If he gets access, we're fucked."

"Relax, Ronin. Let me handle it. It's my ass that will burn if he does that, not yours. You do your job and that's it."

Spencer enters the building downstairs and we go inside and wait for him in the studio, turning on the fans to keep the conversation muddied. Just in case. We are paranoid fuckers and that's why we're not in jail. The keypad on the door beeps out his code and then Spence enters, a little out of breath from running up four flights of stairs.

"Nothing," he says to Ford. "There's a few vagrants down there, that's all."

"I'm not buying it," Ford says. "He's down there, he's just hiding. It's definitely today. He's watching us, waiting for us to fuck up."

"Should we cancel the trip?" I ask Ford.

"Fuck that, we're not canceling the trip," Spencer retorts in a huff. "The sooner we get on the road the better. Keep her confined in the RV. That's better than hanging out here in this huge-ass building. Besides, everyone's ready. The crew are all packed and they'll be here in a few hours."

"Maybe," I say, but internally I'm thinking about all the ways we're sitting ducks inside that RV on that long, almost empty highway leading up to Sturgis. All the way through Wyoming. It's not good.

"You got anything else, Ford?"

"No, it's dead now. Nothing. I got seven proxies to query, though, so I'm gonna go back to Rook's apartment and work on that. Let's just move on like there's nothing out of the ordinary. Pack up the RV, pack up the trucks, when the crew gets here, just keep them busy. We'll decide what to do next on the road."

He walks off towards Rook's apartment and Spencer heads for the door. "I'll be down in the art room packing up the last of my supplies."

I'm like a deer in front of a Mack truck at night. Not sure what to do, paralyzed by the possibilities that are barreling down upon me.

THIRTY-THREE

ROOK

Ronin is a manic mess this morning and I'm standing here in the middle of his apartment, trying for the life of me to figure out why. We're packed, we're on time. The RV is gassed up. The crews aren't here yet, but they're not due for another half hour or so. We ate breakfast. The bike is on the truck. Spence is downstairs getting his supplies together and shutting down the art and production studio.

We're ready. And I'm not even nervous—in fact, I'm looking forward to this trip. I'm gonna get blind-ass drunk up there in Sturgis, I do not even care that I'm underage. I figure if I'm old enough to parade my goods in front of half a million people, a few shots of tequila and some fizzy Coronas aren't gonna make a bit of fucking difference. If I have to sit in the RV and get drunk alone, I will.

The rally officially starts tomorrow, but we're not scheduled for the downtown walk of shame and Shrike Raven unveiling until the day after. It's a long day, one that I'm very anxious to be

MANIC

over. But being naked barely bothers me anymore, I'm so used to wearing nothing that when I do put clothes on for dinner every night, it almost feels weird. I might become a nudist.

I laugh. Right out loud.

Fuck that, I can't wait for winter so I can put on layers of clothes.

"Hey?" I call out to Ronin. He's out on the terrace talking fast and low to Ford, I think. Ford has been texting and calling him all morning. It's starting to drive me crazy because each time Ronin gets more and more wound up. Ronin puts one finger up towards me, then turns and continues his conversation.

Whatever. He's not gonna ruin my trip. I've been stuck in this place all summer, thinking about Jon and all the what-ifs. But he never showed. I figure I'm safe. Ronin was right—he probably did find me, saw I was already involved with someone else, I'd started over and all that, and then he left.

And Ford has been working on the divorce stuff slowly. He tells me a little bit about how we might take care of this every now and then, but he says we should wait until things calm down and then we'll talk about the plan. Annulment, he hints. Sounds good to me. I still run with him every day, it's actually one of the few things in my life that is stress-free and predictable. It allows me to think about nothing for thirty minutes every morning, clear my head. Ford was totally right about exercise. It's good for me.

I can't keep up with him when we run, but he slows down for me a little bit before taking off and going ahead on his own now. He's been talking a lot about the Biker Channel season going through with Spencer, so I've been mulling that over. It sounds a lot better than anything I've ever done, so—

"Rook!"

Ronin comes busting in from the terrace and interrupts my thoughts. "I've gotta go downstairs for a second. Stay here, I'll be right back." He leans down and kisses me on the cheek, then rushes out the door.

"OK," I say to no one, since I'm alone now. I go to the fridge and grab some blackberries from the fruit basket I took from Antoine's office yesterday. I can take or leave his apples and pears, but berries… that's another story.

The doorbell rings and I almost pee my pants, it scares me so bad. I didn't even know we had a doorbell, and for that matter, who the fuck would ring it?

I walk slowly around the corner of the kitchen and then just stare at the door.

Who would ring the doorbell?

I swallow hard as my heart rate picks up.

Who would ring the doorbell?

We're on lockdown, have been for months. No one in or out without a code. Everyone's code was changed when we came back from FoCo after the missing person's report was cleared. And no one who's allowed to be in this building needs to ring the doorbell, because everyone has access to Ronin's apartment via a second code, just in case Jon did come back and somehow make his way inside.

My heart thumps so hard with this thought my hand goes up to my chest. I feel like I have to hold it inside or it will burst through.

It's Jon.

Oh, God. I rush over to my cell phone and push the preset for Ronin. The little icon at the top of the phone says no service.

Oh, fuck.

He's messed up our service.

He's inside the building.

Where can I go?

He must not have the code for Ronin's apartment, either that or he's fucking with me, trying to draw me outside. I tiptoe over to the door and peek through the little peep hole.

There's a sign taped to the wall across from the door.

It says, *Where's Ronin?*

My arms reaches out for the wall before I faint. *Do not faint,*

MANIC

Rook. Do not faint, I tell myself over and over.

He wants me to go outside. It's a trick. I know this, I know it's a trick. I lived with this man for three years, this is how he plays his game. And now that I think about it, that's what that phone call was with Ronin, something to do with Jon.

I stand up and catch my breath. Still, if that freak thinks he's gonna hurt Ronin... I take another deep breath and push my ear to the door. Nothing.

I tiptoe back to the kitchen and grab the biggest knife we have, then walk calmly back to the door.

I twist the handle on the door and cringe as the locking mechanism automatically releases. I wait for the door to burst open, I'm prepared for him to come at me from the hallway.

But nothing happens.

I open the door a crack and wait. Again, nothing.

I throw it all the way open and rush forward into the hallway. Silence and emptiness.

Where the hell is everyone? We're leaving in like half an hour, where's Elise and Antoine?

Oh, God, please, please, I beg. Please do not let them be hurt or worse, dead, by this monster's hand.

I have to stifle down a cry before I remember that my own life is in danger if he catches me. I walk down the hallway, and for once, my old Converse sneakers are the perfect footwear for the job. I stop just before I get to the stairs and push myself up against the wall the way you see people do in the movies, just before they flash their eyeballs around a corner where Charlie's waiting to pump their guts full of lead.

I peek around the corner.

There's a girl down there smoking a cigarette.

"Hey!" I call. "Who the fuck are you?"

She slides her shades down her nose and blows out a ring of smoke. "None of your fucking business. Where's Spencer?"

And then it hits me, this is the other model Spencer used. His ex-girlfriend. "Veronica?"

"Who's askin'?"

I run down the stairs and she spots the knife and starts backing up. "Hey, look—"

"Shhhh," I say. "How the hell did you get in here?"

"Door was open."

"No, the door was *not* open, we're on lockdown."

"It was open," she snorts at me. "And if you try anything with that knife, I've got a gun in my purse and my shooting instructor says I'm the best natural shot he's ever seen."

"You do! Oh, thank God. Get it out, Please. There's a crazy guy in the building, Veronica. He's gonna kill me, please get out your gun!"

"What's going on—"

"Rookie!"

I spin around, the bile in my stomach already exiting my mouth. Green shit splashes across the floor and I cough, my whole body shaking just from the sound of his voice.

"I've been looking for you, baby."

Veronica's backing away from my vomit, screaming obscenities at me.

"Run!" I scream back. And then, because she's got a gun and I don't, I grab her hand and head for the door. She resists for a moment but my panic is contagious. I throw the door open praying that someone, anyone, one of those fucking camera stalkers that have been around all damn summer, is within hearing distance. I scream, "Help!"

I'm still tugging her behind me, but her shock is wearing off as I get to the first landing between the fourth and third floors and she plants he feet firmly on the floor. And I just know, if I save this girl, I'll die. So I yank at her purse as Jon comes into view above us. She resists. "Let go of my purse!" she screams at me. So I let go and run down the stairs, then dash into the art studio. I figure that's where Spencer is, packing up his shit, but when I get in there it's pitch black.

And now I'm trapped.

MANIC

I stumble across the floor, tripping over some light cords, fall on my face, scramble to my feet, and fall again, then settle for crawling towards the back of Spencer's space.

I scramble around the partition that served as my changing room all summer, then lean back against the back wall, desperately trying to silence my gasping breaths. I can hear Veronica and Jon fighting out in the hallway, she's bitching him out, and then a gun goes off and I have to cup my own hand around my mouth to shut myself up.

THIRTY-FOUR

ROOK

The gunshot is still echoing through my ears and the smell of powder invading my nose when I catch the creak of the door opening. I almost shit myself this time. I clamp my mouth shut and pinch one side of my nose together just like that cop did when I had my panic attack.

If I panic now, I die.

I die.

I close my eyes and concentrate on my breathing, listening for footsteps at the same time. I can hear them, but they are not coming towards me, they are walking over towards Director Larry's station.

The lights come on and laughter is blaring through the speakers on the other side of the room.

"*Funny, Rook,*" Ford's voice says.

"*You know what's funnier?*" my voice says. "*The fact that all you dumbasses got the joke. I know what you're reading at night.*"

He's been watching me since I started this job. He's been here

MANIC

since the very beginning. He probably tapped into the camera system. He saw everything, he saw me standing naked in this room, five days a week for the last three months.

A slow clap sounds off from the crew station. "Very nice, Rookie. You look very nice in that bikini. Oh, no wait. That's not clothing, that's *paint*. You're posing nude for these sick freaks. I always knew you were a whore."

The vomit wants to come up again, but I swallow hard and keep very, very still—and I'd like to say quiet as well. But my breathing betrays me. In my own head my breath sounds like a raging tornado. The talking covers up most of it, but it also covers up Jon's footsteps.

I have no idea where he is.

Please, Ronin. Please, please—find me!

"I know you're still in here, Rookie. I'm going to take you home now. We can work this out. Of course, there's a price to pay. And you know, I'm always sorry about that, but you're mine. And you make me do those things. Those terrible, terrible things."

He is closer now. I can't hear his steps, but his voice is near. By the couch Ronin and Ford sit on when I'm being painted. I sit up on my haunches, ready to spring up if he finds me, fisting the knife handle.

Something goes crashing across the room, Spencer's artist lights smashing to the ground, shattering, more things go flying and something hits the partition in front of me.

It shakes.

And he laughs.

"Clever little Rookie. You always tried to hide, but you were never very good at it, were you."

I whimper.

"That's right, love. I've caught you. But I'll make you a deal. You come out and say you're sorry, and I'll wait until we get home to teach you a lesson."

I'm nodding. *What the hell is wrong with me?* I'm nodding! I shake my head and grip the knife harder. Then I stand up.

I can see him over the partition.
He's smiling.
I swallow. "I'm sorry."
"Oh," he laughs. "I'm *sure* you are, Mrs. Walsh. I'm *sure* you are."
He waits to see if I'll say anything else, but I just stand quietly, trying to stay as still as possible.
"Is that it? That's the extent of your apology?" He unzips his pants and points to his crotch.
I swallow hard again and force my feet to move, just far enough to get to the edge of the partition wall. Then I stop and wait.
"All the way over here, *right now!*" He growls out the last two words between clenched teeth.
But I don't move. I know what's gonna happen if I go over there and it won't be anything as simple as a blow job apology.
"Now!" he bellows.
I jump a little in fright, but I stay right where I am and shake my head at him. "No, you're going to hurt me," I say in a shaky voice.
"I came all this way to find you, why would I hurt you, Rookie? I'm not gonna hurt you. Not as long as you apologize correctly."
I take a deep breath and repeat Ford's words in my head. No one can fix this mistake for me, I need to fix it myself. Jon has no right to be here, let alone make demands of me. No right. He's lucky I let him go, not the other way around. He's the dick who abused me, not the other way around. I'm the one with the power of righteousness on my side, not him.
So I count to three, stand up a little straighter, and smile at him.
He smiles back. "That's more like it."
"That's more like it?" I ask. "That's more like it? Look, Jon," I say in my most brave voice as I think up a kick-ass way to really piss him off. I can't take this tension. I can't, I'd rather get it over

MANIC

with. If this is my end, I'd rather just go out fighting like a ballsy street bitch and not whimper and fade away like some pathetic loser. So I force his hand and dig around in my brain for one of my God-given gifts. "I'm real sorry you came all this way to get me, but... even if I were blind, desperate, starved, and begging for it on a desert island, you'd be the last thing I'd *ever* fuck."

His face betrays him. He doesn't know what to do with that remark and I almost laugh. I stole that line from *Scarface* and his dumbass woman-beater brain is struck stupid by it. And then it occurs to me, I've got a million of these movie insults in my head. How many times did I imagine telling this prick off? "And I'll tell you something else, *Jon*, the day I need a friend like you, I'll just have myself a little squat and shit one out." Thank you very much, Frank Darabont and *The Mist*.

And now I do laugh, because that was damn funny.

He charges me, I raise the knife just a second too soon and he sees it, knocks me in the head and sends me flying against Spencer's art supplies. I crash into an art cart, lose hold of the knife, and go sliding across the floor. He picks me up by the hair and starts pulling me towards the exit.

"We're leaving now, Rookie, and you won't be back. So take a good look around and—"

"Just who the fuck do you think you are, you crazy ass-faced bastard?"

Veronica is standing in her ripped-up fishnet stockings, her lipstick smeared, her cigarette dangling out of her mouth, and a bloody gash crossing her billowing white blouse at the waist, like a bullet just missed some very vital organs a few minutes ago.

I laugh again. "Ha! Shoot his ass, Veronica! Shoot him!"

And then shit happens so fast I can't process it. Veronica nods and I can seriously see her finger getting ready to squeeze that trigger when Jon pushes me to the floor and charges her. He hits her dead in the chest, knocking the wind out of her and kicking her ass at the same time, and the gun goes off.

Veronica screams.

My feet know what to do and even though I'm ashamed to leave Veronica there, I scoot around Jon before he can get back on his feet, dash through the door and book it down the stairs.

"Help!" I yell, but this fucking place is totally empty.

Jon is right behind me, only a few steps off actually, and I jump down an entire flight of stairs to the next landing, my exercise with Ford finally paying off, and I gain a few seconds on him. When I get to the first floor I head to the back where the crew should be packing the RV and the vans for our trip. I burst through the first security door and I'm pushing on the long silver bar that will open the second door and take me outside when Jon grabs my shirt and we both go down.

I don't even think, I elbow him in the nose, wince at the sound of cracking cartilage, and I'm back on my feet, stumbling out into the parking lot.

No one. There's no one. I stand there, stupid for a second, then focus on Spencer's truck.

I scramble over to the driver's side door, pull it open and launch myself inside. Jon's got me by the ankles, pulling me back out. And I know, if he gets me out of this truck, I'm dead. I kick out hard and crack him in the mouth with my sneakers.

I reach over and open the glove box, praying that there's a gun in here. I pull out a map and some bullshit papers, my palm searching. I feel the cold hard metal of the weapon, slide my hand around the grip, cock that bitch-ass safety back, then point it right at his face.

"I will blow your motherfucking head off, I swear."

He hesitates and I open the passenger side door, jump down and run back to the building. I'm keying in my code before he comes to his senses and realizes I didn't shoot him. I swing the door open again, running all balls out now, and then smack right into Ronin.

I mow him over and we go down together. Jon catches up, but now he's not worried about me, he's focused on Ronin.

And there's no fucking way this batshit-crazy woman-beater

MANIC

is gonna hurt my new friends.

So I shoot that fucker.

And the gunshot is so loud, it rings in my ears long after Jon falls to the floor, screaming.

THIRTY-FIVE

RONIN

The smoke is still spilling out of the barrel of the revolver in Rook's hand and that psycho rapist is writhing on the floor, his knee blown out and blood pooling under his body. Rook and I are all tangled up and she's shaking uncontrollably as I try to move her aside and figure out what the fuck is going on.

Spencer comes barreling in from the back door, while Ford enters from the front.

"Yes," Ford says into his phone. "I need an ambulance, there's been a shooting at Chaput Studios… "

Rook gasps and looks back at me. I put a hand on her shoulder. "Keep calm, Gidge. I'm not fucking around right now, let me handle this." I hold out my hand. "Give me the gun."

She looks down at the gun, then over to her ex. He's moaning on the ground, blood is still spilling out at an alarming rate.

My little Gidget might've hit an artery.

I smile at that, then turn back to her. "Rook, look at me. We've got about three minutes before the cops get here."

MANIC

She nods her head and hands the gun over.

"You are in shock, OK? Do not say anything. You are in shock. Do you understand me?"

She nods again.

"The whole building is wired, we've got it all on tape. But you are in shock, you will not make a statement until the shock wears off."

I get up and then pull her up along with me.

"Is he gonna die, Ronin?" Her voice is very small and shaky as the reality of what just happened sinks in.

"No, Gidge, we're not gonna let him die. Death is too good for that prick." I take her hand and walk her out the back door. There's people everywhere now. Elise and Antoine are talking to the crew, just getting back from breakfast. Elise is bordering on hysterical, while Antoine catches my gaze and rushes over babbling frantically in French.

"She's OK, she's fine. Let us handle this, Antoine. You two were at breakfast across town, you never saw anything, so step the fuck back and just say *I have no idea* over and over until they get sick of asking you questions."

I open Spencer's truck door and sit Rook down on the passenger side. "Pay close attention, Gidget." She's scared out of her mind right now, so I lean in and kiss her on the head just as half a dozen Denver police pull in the back alley. "You're in shock, remember? Just stay quiet until I'm done talking."

I'm not the genius who perfected this plan.

That's Spencer.

I'm not the hacker who executed this plan.

That's Ford.

I'm the liar who cleans up the mess.

And my job starts now.

"Threatening text messages," I tell the cops. Because that's innocent, really. Easy. And you always want the job to be easy. "If you check his phone, you'll see he sent her text messages this morning, threatening to kill her, me, all of us."

The law about searching cell phones is iffy at best, so we needed a fool-proof way to make sure his phone would be checked on scene—no room for mistakes, no way to hide what he's got on there.

Jon is too smart to send threats by text. But Ford took care of that because sending threats, followed by his genius plan of breaking and entering and attempted murder, means no search warrant is required to access the phone and look for that evidence.

And guess what pops up on the home screen of our friend Jon as soon as the cop swipes his chubby fingers to wake it up?

No really, just guess.

It's almost a giveaway, the Feds use this one all the time. Our version is a new take on the long con bait-and-switch, because we're super-awesome lying, hacking geniuses like that.

Possession of kiddie porn in this day and age is the equivalent of tax evasion last century. That's how they always got the bad guys back then, all those mobsters. Something stupid simple like claiming too many dinners on your taxes.

And let's face it, our boy Jon is one hundred percent guilty of pedophilia, right?

Sure, we set up the photos the cops are confiscating from his phone right now.

But this fuck deserved it.

And believe me, they'll find a whole shitload more at his apartment down the street. Not to mention a transaction, executed less than an hour ago, where he tried to buy more illegal porn, thinking he was purchasing a live cam peek at Rook.

MANIC

I might love Ford right now.

Rook listens carefully as I talk, I can tell. But she keeps her head down and her mouth shut.

"Shock," I say again. "She needs a doctor. Maybe a psychiatrist. He damaged her for years—violent, horrific beatings. Torture. She's not capable of talking right now. We've got a team of lawyers here to make sure she's competent to give a statement."

That shuts down the questioning, because she's not in any trouble here, not at all. All they want is a way to dot the i's and cross the t's so everyone can get the hell out of this parking lot and go grab some lunch.

If you're stupid enough to break into someone's home and attack the occupants in Colorado—and Chaput Studios is most certainly Rook's home at the moment—you're gonna get your ass shot and the person who shot you will never be charged.

Make My Day, it's called.

Make My Motherfucking Day Law. That's what we do with losers like Jon in Colorado when they try to attack us in our homes.

We shoot them. Most of the time we kill them, but Jon deserves his day in court and a very long prison sentence.

He so, *so* deserves that.

And Rook was definitely fearing for her life when she pulled that trigger. She was on the ground, he was coming at her, she was in her home, he broke in.

This is a clear-cut case. It's a textbook case, actually. The cops have no chance of charging her with anything, because we got every second of it on camera.

Of course no one was supposed to get shot. We could've killed him, but that would be way too easy. And not even close to the kind of punishment he deserves. We did underestimate that sick fuck a little because he baited us, got us out of the building chasing after a fake transaction down at Cookie's so he could make his move.

But I think Rook will be OK in the end. She didn't kill him

either, she's not a killer, she's far too sweet for that. She only did what she had to do to protect herself. She should have zero guilt going forward.

The paramedics find Veronica swearing and enraged upstairs and she comes out of the building with her arms around two men as they help her hobble across the parking lot to an ambulance. Her fishnets are a bit ragged from her struggle, she's missing a stiletto, and she's got a trickle of blood running down her side. But her hair's still in place and her cigarette's still hanging out of her mouth. Jon's strapped to a stretcher, ready to be loaded into the ambulance when Veronica passes by. Her fist darts out and she whacks him in the nose. "Bastard," she spits.

You have to love Veronica. You have to. She's like a live-action cartoon character. She's the real-life Jessica Rabbit.

Spencer is a bit shaken that Veronica ended up being involved and he hovers over her as the medics check the flesh wound just above her waist. He's got a weird strained look on his face.

Personally, I think those two are made for each other, but Spencer's not a relationship kinda guy, so Veronica's sorta out of luck.

We could not have planned this part better if we tried because Veronica sucks up attention like it's a precious commodity. She's got the entire parking lot filled with medics and cops twisted around her little finger as she moans about her injury. They all take turns lifting up her shirt to check her flesh wound—scrape really. That bullet scraped her as it flashed past her waist.

Spence catches me watching and smiles at me from across the parking lot, then shoots me with his finger. "We're still road trippin'? Rook? Ronin?"

I look over at Ford. He's busy with the lawyers now, explaining with his hands, smiling, and even laughing a little. The way he always does when things are nearing the end and he knows we just pulled off the perfect job. We're gonna get away with it. Again.

"You wanna stay home, Rook? I think even Ford will

understand if you flake on this deal."

She finally lifts her head and looks me in the eye. "You set all this up?"

I nod. "Well, I came up with the general idea, Spence made it real, and Ford hacked the shit out of that loser all summer trying to get him to take the bait. Of course, I didn't know he had access to the building or I'd never've left you upstairs. I'm so sorry it ended wrong, it was only supposed to be a virtual crime."

She gets a little misty-eyed and I hug her close. "It's over now, OK? It's all over. He's going away, he'll never walk right again, and he's gonna spend a very long time being some thug's prison bitch."

"Thank you," she says in her most serious and sincere voice. "Thank you."

"Any time, Gidge. Any time. Oh, I almost forgot. You might be exactly four hundred and fifteen thousand dollars richer." I laugh as the number rolls off my tongue. "And it might be sitting in non-traceable off-shore bank accounts. Because we might've stolen all his money while we were at it. Serves him right since the only reason he got caught is because he tried to steal yours. Paybacks are always a bitch."

THIRTY-SIX

ROOK

Elise, of all people, is driving the RV up to Sturgis. It's only a six-hour drive, so not a very big deal. But just seeing her tiny hands clutching that huge-ass steering wheel makes me laugh.

"What's funny?" she asks me as she blows past a slow car on the highway. There's hardly anyone on this road. Not many people live up this way. Not many would want to.

"You," I say. "You constantly surprise me, Elise."

A loud roar from the back signals a winner of the current hand of poker. It's just us in this RV—no camera crews allowed. Ford's orders. It's just me, Elise, Spencer, Ronin, Antoine, and Ford. Just us.

My new family.

I cannot even explain how great it feels to think of them this way.

Elise winks at me and then eases the massive vehicle back into the right lane and slows down a little. "I keep everyone on their toes, Rook. If I wasn't here, the whole place would fall

MANIC

down."

I believe that, too.

I chat with her like this for the entire drive, occasionally spotting some wildlife I never even knew existed in the US. Like antelope. Who knew? The cops kept us occupied most of the day yesterday, so we just decided to head out early this morning instead. We still have time to settle in before our show tomorrow. Spencer said he changed his mind about the final painting, he didn't even show Ronin.

I never knew what the original one looked like, so I could care less. This summer I've been sexy Elvis, a cyborg, a slutty hitchhiker, a slutty beach girl, a slutty Catwoman-ish thing… well, just insert slutty in front of all the rest… Fifties waitress, roller derby girl, motocross rider, the tattooed woman—that was cool because Spencer painted me up to match him—rodeo queen, tied-up BDSM rope girl, superhero, go-go dancer, policewoman, mermaid, snow leopard, soccer player and a whole week of slutty lingerie models.

Let me tell you, painting fishnet stockings—the worst. It took the entire day.

But even though I'm still real nervous about the final painting and the show tomorrow night—this has been the best summer of my life. No matter what happens to me, no matter how things go after this is over—whether Ronin and I make it or not—no one will ever be able to take what we created together this summer.

It's very special.

I start to get excited as we get closer because there's lots of other RV's on the road now, plus all the bikers. They come out of nowhere, all of a sudden. One minute we're on this desolate highway in Wyoming, and then, bikers everywhere. All of us heading to the same place. I notice a few motocross racing team transport trucks. "Is there a motocross race here this week?" I ask Elise.

"Yeah," Spencer answers from the seat behind me.

I look back at him.

He winks because he must remember that I told him my first boyfriend was a motocross racer back in Chicago.

I shake my head. "Just asking, Spencer. I was pretty big into it when I was a kid."

"Yeah, good thing, too. Otherwise I'd be teaching you how to ride that beautiful Shrike Rook bike tonight."

I smile and secretly kiss him in my mind for not telling me in front of Elise.

We ease into the campgrounds about an hour later. It's all pretty primitive, but since we're headlining a show, and Spencer needs a private place with access to water in order to paint me, we get to stay in the executive cabins. The big luxury is that it comes with a bathroom.

How lucky are we!

The whole day just flies by with all the settling in. The campground is a madhouse and we're still a few miles outside Sturgis. Ronin and I turn in because I have to get up at three in the morning so Spencer can start painting.

Ronin pulls me up to him in the bed, wrapping his arms around me and kissing my neck. "How you doing, Gidget?"

I turn so I can see his face. "You know, not anything like I should be. I don't understand how I could've shot someone yesterday and today, I'm just camping up in Sturgis like it never happened. And the weirdest thing, Ronin? I could care less. What's that mean?"

He tucks a wayward strand of hair behind my ear. "It means you're gonna be just fine, Rook. You owe that guy nothing. Not one second of remorse or sympathy."

"Yeah," I sigh. "That's what I figure too. I'm just gonna forget about it, Ronin. I'm just gonna let the past go, move forward with you."

MANIC

He squeezes me. "You make my heart happy right now, Rook. So totally and completely happy."

We cling to each other, but not in a desperate way. We cling to each other and fall asleep in a way that makes us feel complete.

And when stupid Ford comes pounding on our cabin door at 3AM, I wake up feeling complete as well.

"OK, Rook, last painting."

Ronin and Ford went to the campground general store to get coffee for everyone, so right now it's just Spencer and I in his cabin. He's moved the beds out of the way to give us room, and he's got the music going. I'm pretty sure no one in this campground but Ronin and I bothered to go to sleep, because the party is still raging outside. It's loud as fuck and if I wasn't such a heavy sleeper, that might've prevented me from getting some shut-eye. But as it happens, I can sleep through the Sturgis rally no problem.

"Are you gonna tell me what it is?"

"Nope!" he says, grinning like a teenager. "You'll just have to discover it as I go."

He gets his airbrush out and a smoky gray color goes on first. I watch patiently as he winds the paint around my body in ribbons. He switches to another airbrush so he doesn't have to keep cleaning it between colors and sprays on some black, blending it together. After that there's more gray, some shades lighter, some shades darker, and white to bring it all together. Even though he's only done background colors, it already looks amazing.

Ronin and Ford come back with the coffee and take a seat on the couch to watch, but even with the caffeine and the roaring sounds of motorcycles outside, not to mention Spencer's airbrush, neither of them last long because Spencer is building the scene in a really cryptic way to keep us all guessing.

It becomes too boring for the tired babies and they are out.

It's late morning before I figure it out, that's how well-honed Spencer's craft is. He's applying the red, the only other color besides the shades of black, gray and white, when it all starts to click.

"It's us."

Spence shoots me with his finger, just like he did when he sat across from me in Cookie's and offered me this job all those months ago. "It's you two. It was a helluva summer, huh, Rook?"

"Yeah, it really was. But you know what, Spencer? I'm so glad I did this with you. My whole life has changed and you're a big part of it."

"Same here, Blackbird. Same here. We got the contract for the first season of Shrike Bikes. It's your job, but I'll live if you say no."

"I'll talk to Ronin and see."

When Ronin and Ford wake up they are stunned silent by the artwork on my body. It's all in shades of black and red, just like Spencer's tattoos, and the front piece is a beautiful composition depicting a Samurai warrior and a blackbird sitting in a cherry tree. For the first time, in all the paintings Spencer Shrike has competed on my naked body, my girly parts are not emphasized. The painting flows flawlessly over my curves, hiding every inch of skin underneath. The blossoms take me back to the first day I arrived at Chaput Studios, broken, scared, and barely holding myself together.

And a gentle man named after a masterless warrior pushed me in a swing and started the healing.

But that moment in time was fleeting, just like those flowers.

That girl blew away in the wind and this girl took her place.

MANIC

If I thought the catsuit made me feel beautiful and fully dressed, this is a hundred times that.

I feel like a goddess.

And when I get to town, I walk down that Sturgis strip with my head up, feeling loved and pretty.

And no one whistles or talks to me rudely. They say hello, they compliment Spencer's talent, they take pictures with me, and they treat me like a piece of art.

I see him in the crowd. Watching me, following our progress down the street, but from the opposite side. Trying to be stealthy, I guess. And a small part of me wonders if he's the real reason I took this job so quickly. I knew as soon as I saw the motocross transport trucks on the highway he'd be here. So did Spencer.

He comes to the show that night too. Stands right in front. Here the crowd is more rowdy, they are all drunk after all, but Wade stands still, his eyes never moving from me while I'm on stage.

He was my first love. I thought he was the one. I cried over losing him for years after his mom sent me away.

But when he finally lifts his hand to wave I don't wave back.

Because I'm not a runner anymore.

I'm a chaser.

END OF BOOK SHIT

I loved writing Manic. I loved imagining Spencer painting those bikes up in Antoine's studio. I loved the fact that Rook wanted to run with Ford, even if she didn't understand why. I love the fact that Rook brought the team back together after being mad at each other for years.

The story is only starting so I can't give away too much, but in Panic the stakes are raised. Not just for Rook and Ronin and their developing relationship. But for all the team members.

So here's something I never told anyone about this R&R series. I love movies about con jobs. It started when I was like ten and I first saw The Sting. And ever since then I was just enthralled with "smart criminals". And the ultimate movie about con men, for me at least, was Ocean's Eleven. I fucking loved that movie because I love when the bad guys are so compelling, you can't help but root for them.

This gang here, they are bad guys. They were written in a way that should make you root for them, but they are all bad guys. Even Rook, as you will see in Panic, has her moments of unscrupulous behavior. They all have a past. They all have crimes they've committed. They all have transgressions.

And yet... they are likeable.

Just like Ocean.

It fascinates me. I really wanted to understand why I was rooting for criminals in Ocean's Eleven. So I thought about it a lot as I wrote this series and I came to the conclusion that there are no good guys in life. I mean, yeah, a few gentle souls are born each year who really are "good". But they are not the norm. Most people make mistakes. Most people need a second chance at one time or another. And most people can appear to be good when paired up against a "badder" person.

Good and bad are relative. So if you pair a character up with an entity who is "badder" than them, they suddenly become the good guys.

That's why we rooted for Ocean. His quest was to win back his girl from the greedy casino owner. Plus, Ocean was devoted to his team and went to jail rather than turn them in.

In other words, Ocean was likable, he was loyal, and in the end, he was smarter than anyone gave him credit for.

That's why I liked him. He outsmarted everyone.

This team here, they are smart too.

They are smarter than they look.

They are stronger together than they are alone.

And they are loyal to the end.

Thanks for reading and I'll see you at the end of Panic.

Julie

Printed in Great Britain
by Amazon